Pr

It has been rumored that there is a book, so sinister, so macabre, that it floated down the River Styx, before rising to Earth. The origins of such a work have been the discussion of many historians. The book has been the subject of legend for many years. No one has determined its author. Within its pages are stories so bizarre, that it is believed to be written from the deepest, blackest, chambers of the mind. A war on any reader's psyche. It is believed that whoever opens the book, usually goes into a state of hypochondria; a meltdown of sorts, fueled by the very stories within.

My dear friend, if you are reading this now, then you have stumbled upon the work. You are about to step into a world of evil and mystical realms. You will be teleported into the darkest corners of the heart. Do not utter its name. For it is said that whoever speaks the title, will be subject to another entry into: *the Dead Diaries.*

What do you see

When the darkness comes?

I see you

Laying in an oversized grave

What do you feel

When the darkness consumes?

The emptiness of a thousand

Words left unsaid

What do you see

When the reaper appears?

I see an ocean

Of cemeteries

Dragging me in.

Dead Diaries

By Austin German

To J:
~~Scream~~! Read! Bloody horror!

Hamburger Man

Out of the eater, something to eat; out of the strong, something sweet.

- Judges 14:14

1.

You see there is this longing inside of me. A force of wind that twists and turns. A rage filled with desire and hope. It spins underneath this shell. I stare up into the starlit sky, how they remind me of fireflies. Their radiance so pure, so phenomenal that I can feel them burning. That's when I remember it. I remember the burning. This calling that begins to rush through me. I see you. I see the ones who think they're safe. The ones who demand justice but offer none. The ones who mock and degrade their bodies. The sinners that have run rampant across this land. This longing is to purify the regions. Purify them from their senseless acts of destruction. I know their kind. How they are so tormented. Let me give you peace. That is why I do what I do. I must save you from your emptiness. For in these final moments of blood, you shall attain a profound peace. I see you in the shopping malls. You idolize others and without hesitation cough up cash, as if your bowels are made directly from the Federal Reserve.

You conform because you are so terrified of being cast out. Yet you cast others out who are different from you, but the same as you. Me, I am not you. I see beyond these shallow graves you dig. Every day you pile more dirt on without even realizing how sunk in you truly are. A coffin maker, you create your own demise and then grow ignorant right before the slaughter. That is where I begin. You look at me and see a man. I am no man. I am no homosapien. You look at me and what do you see? You see a monster. You look at my hands and see a monster. I am no monster. I look at my palms and see a liberator. This is what it means to be a savior. This is how I came to realize that you all look so beautiful on the stove.

2.

Julie Mears stood nude before her bathroom mirror. Sweat was slowly dripping down the elegant portions of her body. Her blonde hair with blue tips was clustered in all different directions. This was the sixth time she succumbed to her impulse, to her instant gratification. It was fifty-fifty in her mind to make this time the last or keep going. She turned away from her reflection and bent to turn on her shower. The pipes in the wall gargled until a stream of water splashed out into the tub. Over the roar and echoing of the running water, she did not hear her phone ring from the other room.

Kyle Herdon opened his eyes from slumber. He heard water trickle into his consciousness. He sighed heavily, the sex had once again been amazing. A smile of ecstasy spread from ear to ear. A bedside lamp erased the blackness of the room. He stared up at the ceiling. A poster of Leonardo Di'Caprio peered back at him. Julie's studio was small and only the bed with a nightstand and a futon furnished it. A TV hung on the wall in front of the bed. He reached for the remote when Julie's cellphone began to ring. He rolled over and glanced at the caller ID. It was Julie's sister Katie, his girlfriend.

A rush of disappointment and adrenaline sped through Kyle's body. This was much too close to getting caught. His eyes stayed transfixed on the front of the iPhone. On the screen the call ended and a text box appeared. *Call me it's about grandma,* it read. The sisters' grandma had been in the hospital for almost three weeks due to falling down. She had tumbled down stairs and hit her head. Kyle had to hear Katie every night cry and be filled with despair. Grandma Judith had been her favorite and the two were very close. He tore the brown comforter off his naked self, and hustled over to the bathroom. He banged loudly. The shower stopped and after a couple seconds, Julie poked her head out. Steam exited the crack in the door. "What?" she asked, as her head trembled slightly. She was already getting cold. He stared at her a moment and thrusted the phone towards her, "Katie called. She sent you a text too. It's something about Judith. She wants you to call her." She retrieved the phone from him and sank back into the steam clouds of the bathroom. When the door was shut all the way, Kyle hurried over to get dressed. Katie would soon be coming home from teaching dance.

Julie sat on the toilet with the lid closed and a beige towel wrapped around her middle. A lime green towel was piled atop her head like a cupcake swirl. Another towel separated her bottom from the plastic lid underneath her. She was wasteful and consuming. She didn't care. This would be the first time she ever talked to her sister while Kyle was there. The cheating had transpired only eight weeks ago. Even though Kyle and Katie had just finished their three year anniversary. Julie did not know why she had been sleeping with him. Things sort of just happen. Kyle was a straight up player. She knew she was being used for her abilities during sex, but she secretly hoped that he would pick her over her sister eventually. He was super handsome with a jet black comb over that sat perfectly on his head. His mesmerizing aqua eyes sat deep within his skull. Her intuition sought out to tell Katie, but she still kept the secret guarded in her heart. Looking down at her phone she found Katie's number and waited as the familiar rings droned. Maybe old Judith had recovered, but Julie doubted it. Katie picked up the line, her sister could hear the sniffles uncovering her crying. "Julie, grandma passed away," Katie said between broken sobs. Julie's hand shook as she held the phone to her ear. She hated hearing her sister like this. Maybe it was time to stop, to lay it all out on the line.

"When's the funeral?" she asked.

"In four days. Mom is flying from California, but we...we should drive. It's just to Phoenix."

"In whose car?" Julie asked. She herself was carless.

"Mine; it's more reliable than Kyle's, but hopefully he'll drive. I'm devastated."

Julie was silent. She listened to her sister sob. She wanted to cry too. But not for dear grandma Judith. She was feeling the convictions of the affair. But she wasn't dating her sister's boyfriend. Just fucking him. No, that was wrong; just as wrong as going on dates. Julie wanted to throw up.

"Katie, when this all passes, there's something really important I have to tell you. Don't push it right now, let's focus on Judith. But I will tell you when I'm ready. Okay?"

"Are you in danger? Did the store fire you?"

"No. Now listen, nothing like that. So Wednesday we'll head out? Get to Phoenix a day before the funeral?"

"Yes, Julie," her sister sniffed and whimpered. They hung up. Nothing more to be said. She opened the bathroom door and saw Kyle tying his shoes. At least he was leaving. She looked him straight in the eyes.

"It's over, it's so fucking over," she said. Suddenly, he leaped from his seat on the bed. His shoes fully tied, he grabbed Julie by her mouth with his index, and middle finger inside, gripping the bottom of her chin and jaw.

"I'll tell you when it's over!" he roared. Kyle pushed her against the wall. She fell to the floor. Her naked body looked so fragile. She was such a beautiful woman. Her nakedness made him want her again and again. Instead, Kyle opened her door letting himself out. He walked into the hallway of the apartment complex. His phone rang. Julie stood up and peeked out of her door. She knew it was Katie. She heard him say, "I was getting ice cream." What a liar. Only a five to six hour drive remained between the two.

In a few days they would be traveling from Bluff, Utah. To Phoenix, Arizona. Then she would end it. She would tell her sister everything. She would spill the beans anyway possible.

3.

My parents divorced and my mother left the country. Scared of my father, my mother was. She got the courts to give her parents, my grandparents, full custody of me. Maybe she knew something then; maybe she knew who my father truly was. But maybe not. I guess I'll never know. I don't fully understand why she didn't take me with her. Well, it's all in God's hands. As a child I never fit into the culture of grade school, or felt the agony of high school. I never knew what it felt like to be popular or kick a football. You see the first time I was bullied I took a baseball bat from the P.E room. I snuck up on my bully while on recess. I whipped that bat through the air colliding with my aggressor's back. He fell breathing irregularly and oceans poured from his eyes. I had strategized a plan all along. Before going to school I had stolen my grandpa's fishing knife. Now I extracted it out from my pocket and with my foot pining his arm and hand, I began to cut his digits off. I managed to get three fingers off his right hand before his screams of anguish brought a teacher to his aid. Blood was everywhere and I knew I loved it. I felt that I had done nothing wrong. He had to learn his lesson. He was my first taste as to what a sinner's blood tastes like. You see, I took one of his disposed digits and stuck it in my mouth. I sucked on the skin and smiled a big bloody mouth smile. The teacher was horrified. After this ordeal I was deemed too dangerous to stay with my grandparents, let alone keep going to this school. The courts got in touch with my father, finally. At first he didn't want me; said it was better off if he never knew me or saw me again. But then the Lord gave him a dream. A dream that together he and I could fulfill the commands of our Lord.

So I was sent out to the middle of nowhere on the Arizona reservation between Rough Rock and Kayenta. The land was sparsely populated. It was perfect cover for our mission. Here is where my father had been practicing and doing the Lord's work. I was ten years old when I went to live with him. When I arrived I could tell instantly that a connection had been made. The kind where you look into someone's eyes and you telepathically say "I know who you are. What you are." It was a feeling of perfection. I was with someone who knew that longing inside of me. He could relate to it. My father had a lucrative fencing business. He had supplied all the fencing along the farms and the highways. He also had a subsidy in the cattle business. This angle would prove beneficial when the time came for the meat. I learned all of it. I was to inherit the cattle anyway. The house was good too. A one story, three bedroom house with a basement. That was our holy chambers where we took the sinners. That room was where I learned of my calling and my duty. In the beginning I was scared but my father had a little black book he said was the bible. He read from it every day to me. Morning and night. In it was scripture, guidelines and recipes. This is where my revolution would begin, where I found out that you all look so beautiful on the stove.

My father spoke of sacrifice. How everyday it was up to us to sacrifice our desires to fulfill our calling. As I grew I realized that my calling was my desire and my desire was my duty. He would bring me impure sinners. First it was women. These people had offered themselves to us sexually for the money in our wallets. How disgustingly sick is that? If our body is the Lord's temple, which my daddy says it is, you shouldn't defile it in such ways. Only if it was for procreation. Never just pleasure. So I learned how to liberate them. I liberated them first in the basement and then gave them peace on the stove. I was never timid when the day of reckoning came, the time of purification by death. I placed hands on them, not sexually of course, but firm. Stern like a scolding parent. But these were not my offspring. Just humans that needed the ultimate release. They were bound and drugged, completely naked on our offering stone. My father said that nakedness was needed so they could enter the afterlife without any possessions or prejudice. That once naked they were all the same. So we took our ceremonial knife and bled them. Other times we just used our hands because that was fulfilling to feel the life beneath our palms. It was a rhythm to my heart. I would smile at my father and he would smile back. Sometimes he would work long hours at the fencing warehouse or the cattle plant, but always had time to teach me our true work. To show me the ways of our Lord. The sinners' release took time and careful preparation. Nothing was ever rushed; it was very intimate. Sure the drugged up sinner would scream or beg. I often petted them telling them that this is the only way to find peace. That liberation is what's best for them.

They couldn't understand that this release was needed. Fleas and ticks do not understand the harm they cause. But an infestation of such creatures is horrid. My acts against this species was not horrid, but about control. About giving them the release they sorely needed. To this day I look at them, all the ones who passed through my side of the reservation. None were happy, all were synthetic. All were like little ants following blindly. Following each other into more slavery. I have to save them. Don't you understand? I have to give them their release. That's all that matters to me. They need to let me do it. Humans behind badges and ones that hide behind miserable banks kill every day. You go to war and slaughter every country because big corporations sleeping with banks tell you to. Cops can shoot whoever they want, but I guarantee the judge will want to kill me. So why is what I'm doing any different? Because your laws say it is? Because the masses see a monster when they hear my name or see me? But I will never say sorry. For I am not sorry. I will give you all the release you need. The ultimate moment that will lead you to my stove, where daddy taught me all the perfect recipes.

4.

Four days later the pretend-happy couple were loading bags and suitcases into the trunk of Katie's Camry. Katie had cried all night and into the morning. All Kyle could distinguish between sobs, coughs, and tears is that she loved Judith. Now for the first time she was silent. Angry at Kyle for barely even holding her. He showed hardly any remorse for the death of her family member. He was acting distant, and it was making her discouraged. She had sensed something weeks ago, but of course whenever she confronted him on it they would end up fighting. She wanted to feel loved again, but his pride and his coldness were erasing more feelings for him day after day. He kissed her occasionally but their sex life had gone from one hundred percent to about twenty-five. Even she thought, being twenty-nine years old, that this was ridiculous and that something was wrong. Her anger was billowing up inside of her like smoke in a chimney. A fire that she quickly needed to put out if she didn't want to slip back into how she used to be.

Now she watched him place the luggage into the trunk. He smiled at her and nodded in approval that it was okay for him to drive. A smile. What a dirty way of pretending to show interest or affection. She decided to smile back, to let the time pass by. Suddenly, a bike bell rang, startling her before she could get into the Camry. Julie was riding up on her bicycle ringing the damn bell on her handlebars repeatedly. Katie watched her sister get off the bike and head towards her. She had a single backpack strung upon her shoulders. Katie gave Julie a hug. "Hi sis, ready for the road?"

"Yeah, let's get this over with. I'm going to put my bike in your apartment. Is that cool?"

"Yes. Just put it right there in the hallway," replied Katie. Julie handed Kyle her backpack.

"This is all you brought?" he asked. She ignored his remark and started for the building. Kyle tossed her bag into the trunk and closed its top.

"Hey wait up, I'll help you with the bike," he cried chasing after Julie.

Katie slipped into the passenger seat and turned the engine over on the car. She stared diligently at her sister and boyfriend. Hastily, the pair disappeared into the apartment. Kyle closed the door and grabbed Julie by the wrist spinning her around, directly after she placed her bike against a wall. The sudden weight and movement caused the pictures above the bicycle to rattle. He held her tightly and glared at her.

"Just stay silent and this will all pass. No need to get her more upset."

"Let me go, asshole."

"I have a better idea for that," he said.

"You're disgusting, I told you no more."

"Wrong. I will continue to screw both of you as I see fit."

"You're insane. What the hell's the matter with you?"

"It's all in the family," he said, smiling a big smug grin. He let go of her wrist, and she snapped her arm away. Julie flipped her hair and ran into the summer air. She wanted desperately to stay home now and just tell her sister the truth. But Kyle was right, her sister's emotions were as wide as the Grand Canyon. No need to split her apart any harder, at least not yet. She rolled up her sleeves on her brown checkered flannel and climbed into the backseat of her sister's car.

"You okay? What happened, Julie?" her sister asked.

"Nothing, I just hate your boyfriend, always have and always will."

That part was true. Up until she saw him naked. Everything had happened so fast that day. She had gone over to the apartment to drop off the keys for the Camry for her sister. Of course she had the apartment keys so she let herself in. Someone was in the shower. She knew that it wasn't her sister. But curiosity was tugging at her. Plus, she wanted to tell him where she had left the car keys and not to forget to pick her sister up from work. So she maneuvered down the hallway to the bathroom door. It stood ajar and she took the bait. Carefully and quietly she opened it further to discover Kyle naked. There was no curtain, just glass that had fogged over in certain places. In the places that were transparent, she saw taut thighs. A muscular abdomen and his pecs were perfect and they were moving. He was breathing in an odd way as his arm and hand kept going up and down. Suddenly she saw what he was fondling and doing. He looked up surprised, but then said in the most nonchalant tone, "Are you just going to look at it? Or would you like to touch it?" She crept in and saw that it was more impressive than she thought. Why did she do it? It was pure lust, almost animalistic. But it had been fantastic to feed on impulse. Love was not existent. She didn't believe in love at all.

"Let's just get through this trip. For Grandma Judith, okay?" Katie said as she placed a hand into her sister's.

"Yes Katie. I'll do my best."

Now Kyle was in the car. The girls fell silent as he slid the vehicle into reverse and then into drive. The silver four door car sped off onto Eighth Avenue. They were heading south onto the highway. It felt good to be leaving Utah Katie hoped for a nice getaway. Maybe this is what her relationship needed. Maybe it could help strengthen their bond. If it didn't, which she expected it not to, perhaps she would just call it quits. Being almost thirty next year, and with no kids did feel like she was missing something; that she had no meaning in life yet. Either way she was going to try to enjoy herself and mourn for her grandma. She knew Judith would have given her great advice, for all grandparents knew wisdom beyond their years.

5.

I was eighteen years old when you took my father away from me. By now in the course of eight years we had liberated twelve women together. Separately, I am not sure how many he had done before I came to live with him. My father was a smart man, almost ingenious in every way possible. But time was catching up with him; his oldness started to appear. Some days it wouldn't show, then rapidly like lightning he would forget things. He would stammer or fall down. Days like this, instead of liberating, he would show me how to cook. How and where to separate the flesh. Once the skin was off the bone, he taught me how to carve it. We had beautiful sculptures made out of bone. Just thinking about it now makes my own skin tingle. I hope if I am ever captured that my art will be preserved. Anyway, the days that he was smart he told me he had a plan for me. There were two possible routes from this point forward. He secretly knew that we might get caught eventually. Either together, or apart. If it was to be together, I was to fake my death. If it was separate, then I was to inherit the cattle farm.

I remember descending the stairs to our holy chambers. As I mentioned before this is where we gave each sinner their peace. I knew an Asian whore was down there bleeding out. But I didn't know that my father had forgotten to secure her hands. Only her ankles had been bound. This sinner escaped and found one of our tools. She rushed on me, went up on the stairs and stabbed me in my left shoulder. I still have the scar. I couldn't believe it! She had the audacity to use our own tools of holiness, to stab me. Filth! How I wish I could have given her release. Her hair was so pretty. I needed it for our wreath on our front door. So this sinner stabbed me and managed to get by me. I fumbled down the stairs. She escaped our grasp that day. The date was June tenth, nineteen-ninety-seven.

When the authorities came, my daddy and them had a marvelous shoot out. He had a plan though. Remember, he knew it would happen. On Monday of that week, so that would have been two days before this dilemma, my dad had given release to a boy my age. He had kept it a secret from me until now. He began to scream at me to get the body out of the sanctuary of the basement and take it to my room. As I completed this task my father took gasoline to the whole house, as the police were making their way across our acreage in the front. He lit our house on fire with a single match. As the walls, curtains and possessions burned, I noticed happiness on my daddy's face. He handed me his black book, our bible. He told me how proud he was of me and that it had been an honor serving in the legion with me. He gave me a farewell kiss and said to go to the rendezvous point. Then he lit himself on fire. I split out the back and hid amongst the brush and trees for a while. I watched as my home burnt to ash. Everything I had learned and everything we had done was billowing up into the sky. I was happy I had been homeschooled and that I had lived with my dad. I was happy I made him proud. On this day I realized it was time to become him. A better version of him though. It would take time. With the house gone and two bodies found so far, and all the other bodies yet to be discovered, the authorities were perplexed. The body of the boy had resembled me and all his fingers had been chopped off. The authorities knew my dad had been a killer, what you call a serial killer. A psychopath. So they just assumed he had tortured me. So faking my death was an excellent idea. The government, the police, everyone wanted to sweep this mess under the rug. I only regret I wasn't able to roast my decoy or any of the pigs. I bet they would have all looked beautiful on my stove.

I managed to get to the rendezvous point. An old forgotten run down motel with a destroyed gas station out front. It sat off of Interstate 160. I followed my father's instructions precisely. The motel only had six rooms. In the second one, buried under the bed beneath the floor boards, I found his briefcase with two-hundred-thousand dollars. It was with this money that I became who I am today. I realized that I didn't need electricity for I built my own stove, my own kiln out back. I would work by daylight and the night gave me comfort. I became one with the land. I used some of the money to fix up one of the motel rooms. I mostly stayed out of sight. But soon I left the nest and began my journey. I learned how to hide myself and my identity. Always only paying in cash and never drawing attention to myself. At first as I began to go out on my own to liberate, I was frightened. It was more of nervous fear. I wanted to do it right. It felt strange to me when I was amongst the sheep, amongst the sinners. I could sense them staring at me almost as though they knew I was their predator. But then I realized they were fools; they stare because they're judging. They are scrutinizing every aspect of me and everyone else except themselves. I mean you all wear the same clothes, listen to the same music and watch all the same shows. Why does the news matter? Why does any of it matter? Alas, it doesn't, it creates the propaganda your species thrives on. Thank my Lord I am not like you scum at all. I hate it! I hate it all so much, but I know I will be rewarded for my deeds. My daddy never lied to me and what he says is truth. So as I began to grow into my own version of my father, I discovered that women are not the only sinners. In my dad's bible I read a passage that said when I was older and ready, I would see other men with men, sexually. They needed to be released along with the others who had disgraced their bodies. Soon, even though it wasn't written in the book, I took to hating all your kind and decided that you all need saving. Any race, any sex, any age, all of you were needing release. The prowl had begun. There was no turning back now. I dove right in to my father's black book. The guidelines were given by our Lord. The recipes were to be followed exactly.

The seasons and years passed and my obsession of salvation was escalating fast. In the first three years I took it relatively slow, but it was building. Cellphones ruined a lot of my calling and I had to learn very fast how to dispose of them and the cars. Those damn vehicles were the hardest part. As your species rushed into the new millennium everything could be tracked. I hate cellphones, I hate computers. My wrath is my savior's wrath and I use it justly to administrate the peace. I would stalk the tourists at Four Corners, or the fairs. Hell, everyone hitchhikes up here. I picked them up and gave them salvation. I was running out of money but I had a plan. A plan that lead to the truth of absolute vengeance. Your society is all about food and instant gratification. I knew I loved the taste of sinner, but what about sinners eating sinners? It was a truth that led to the stove where the recipes changed the face of roadside food forever. The stove never looked so beautiful.

6.

The heat from the summer sun rained down onto the Camry in a tide of fire. The temperature of the waves was so discomforting that Julie had tied her flannel into a knot below her breasts, exposing her stomach. Her slender legs were spread as she sat sideways. She had one leg up on the center console of the car. Inside, the air conditioner was blowing relief and at this angle, the air hit all the right places. Katie peered out into the accelerating wilderness. The desert was dry, disgustingly hot and unflattering. After a few moments she turned away from the window and stuck her head right in front of the dash vent. Her brown hair flowed upon her bare shoulders as it wisped above her halter top. She wished she would have worn shorts. Kyle kept his hands on the wheel and seemed to be the only one not bothered by the weather. She did notice he had gallons of sweat stains camouflaging his white t-shirt. He examined his rearview mirror and caught a glimpse of Julie. He took one hand off the wheel and angled the mirror in a small downward motion.

"Keep your eyes on the road, please," instructed Katie. "Slow down too."

"Do you want to drive?" was her boyfriend's response.

"No, but honestly this isn't Nascar."

He kept his lead foot heavy on the gas pedal. "I don't need any side seat driver. We're going to get there."

"Yes, but I'd like to be all in one piece," she said.

Julie listened carefully. The couple had fought twenty-five minutes ago about something as stupid as food. They were all hungry but Kyle insisted they keep going. They were three hours in, with three more to go. Katie let out a huff of disgust.

"Please, just slow down, I don't want to get pulled over," she said.

Before Kyle had time to respond Julie butted in. "Stop fighting! Can't you guys go one hour without bickering?"

"Now, I especially don't need a backseat driver," growled Kyle. He sped up and passed a slow moving RV. He had the Camry going about twelve miles over the posted limit.

"Screw you, Kyle!" shouted Julie.

"Really? That sounds like a lot of fu-"

Katie cut him off. "Look, just try to relax; it's too hot for this."

"Yes, yes it is," said Kyle, as he angled the rear view all the way down, exposing Julie. He was becoming flustered and hot. But he was boiling not because of the sun, but because of the heat inside his blood. He could almost see up inside her shorts. He continued to stomp down on the gas, his speed gaining momentum with every beat of his heart. He gulped and tried to tell his third leg to calm down. No one saw the coyote begin to cross their path of travel. It stalked slowly as his skinny body and padded feet met the asphalt. Kyle kept his eyes transfixed on Julie. He had begun imagining what any thirty-year old man would. Suddenly Katie screamed, waking him from his stupor. He over corrected the car and just barely missed the hind end of the animal. The trio flew off the highway and into the shoulder. They began to race over into the desert. Nature's dust flew up on all sides of the vehicle as if the Camry was surfing on a blanket of sand. They collided with a wooden barbwire fence. The passenger tire hit the obstacle hard, and Katie could feel the rubber run over the wood. Immediately the tire pressure warning chimed. Julie screamed as Kyle maneuvered back onto the highway. He cursed and banged his hands onto the steering wheel. "Stop that! Don't hit my car!" yelled Katie. He glared over at his girlfriend; now all of his blood was rushing into a tsunami of adrenaline. But instead he restrained himself. "That's the least of our worries, sweetie." Julie managed to finally catch her breath. She was furious, "What the fuck's the matter with you? Are you trying to kill us? Are you? What is the matter with you? Keep those stupid eyes of yours on the road or I'm driving."

Kyle Herdon slammed on the brakes so hard that both girls lurched forward. He stopped on the shoulder and jumped out of the Camry. Katie followed him, yelling at the top of her lungs. Julie swore her sister could have been on "The Voice" with a vocal range like that. She got out of the car to watch the pair squabble. She almost wished she had some popcorn. After she realized the intensity of the sun again, she broke up the fight.

"Give me the keys," she demanded. Her sister fell silent. Kyle looked confused.

"Why?" he asked.

"Because I'm driving now; both of you are too unstable."

Ignoring her sister, Katie walked over to the passenger tire. Sure enough a piece of barbwire was lodged into the exterior, penetrating its interior.

"See! See Kyle, we have to call a tow truck now! The tire's going to be shot!"

"Relax babe, I'll just change it right now. You do have a spare and a jack in the trunk right?"

"No, Kyle I do not. Should I just pull one out of my ass? Where's Robin Williams when you need a genie? Oh yeah, he's dead. Just like we're going to be!"

"You're kind of overreacting. I'm sure there's a place up further."

"Really, you want to drive on this?" asked Julie, as she pulled her phone out of her pocket.

"What if the barbwire is holding air in?" said Katie.

Julie watched as her sister continued to strut around the car. Julie said, "I have no signal." Katie and Kyle both checked their phones. No bars. Katie opened her door and said, "Fine, let's drive until we get a signal. It's too hot for this crap." Her sister and boyfriend quickly and quietly, got back into the car. All were silent, *well that settles that,* thought Kyle.

The Camry now went the proper speed limit. The trio was silent as they drove farther into the reservation. The A/C was on blast and it felt nice, but did little justice to the harsh Arizona sun. Julie always wanted to go past Phoenix. She had read that there really was a fence between the U.S and Mexico. Katie opposed the idea. She would know; she did go to school in Yuma. When she had gotten back to Utah after her final year in high school, she told Julie it got to be one-hundred-nineteen degrees. Julie thought that was impossible until she looked it up herself.

"Can I turn on some of my tunes?" she asked, as she plugged her phone into the Aux port.

"Is it that metal crap?" asked Katie.

"Yes."

Katie sighed but nodded her head. After all her sister was driving and she was enjoying just looking out the window. The blurring scenery flew by in a cosmic brownish green haze. Katie thought this surely resembled her life. Lately everything had been up in the air, flying around like some sort of tornado. Her yoga and her ballet class did give her spirit renewed energy. She loved teaching ballet. That was by far the best part of her life at the moment. Julie had put on the band Disturbed. Great, Katie thought to herself, *now I have to listen to someone gargle at the beginning of each song.* She grew tired of the whirlwind of nature and turned to talk to Kyle. He was asleep, quite dead to the world in the backseat. After a few songs passed, Julie turned down the music and looked at her sister sitting next to her. She looked solemn, glum. Julie glanced out the window and decided to try to converse.

"No cacti, pretty weird, huh," she said.

"Nope, but there's a lot where I went to school."

"I'm sorry I know that was hard for you. A rough time and everything."

"But you didn't almost kill a teacher, Julie."

"But I would have, if he had done the same to me. Hell, you got pretty close."

"Not close enough."

7.

Let me take it back a little bit now that I am contemplating on these recipes. You see when my father and I would go out in public and eat at restaurants or bars I would be among the sinners. These stages of my journey were truly hell. If we had wanted to, he and I could have liberated every soul in these establishments. But our hands would liberate later, when the opportune moment presented itself. As I sat amongst them, I learned their mannerisms. I watched intently as they moved, spoke, walked and behaved. Why is it that you people think you're so much better than the ones next to you? Why does arrogance overrun your cup of life? There were always one or two of the sinners thinking they were above everyone else. And how you treat each other! Your actions are so repulsive.

But I know that there are many forms of slavery. I see my flock of sinners, slaves and the fools. Do not fret, I am here to save you. The burning is still buried deep within my pulse. Now back to the recipes. You see there were two things my daddy always had on his person at all times. His black book which was the bible. This book I inherited. The second item he always carried was a small baggie with sinner's meat. The meat contained inside was ground up so small, that everywhere we went to eat, he sprinkled it onto our dish. In so doing we had the pleasure of our meat mixed in with the rest of our food. Here is where the recipes were born.

Now back to the present. Of course, I had obtained my father's perfect cooking skills. I got the best tasting meat in the county by mixing the sinners' leftovers with the cattle from my father's farm. As the years progressed my funds began to deplete, as I knew it would happen. So on certain weeks of the month I would open up a roadside hamburger and beef stand. The stand would be strategically placed at different intervals along the highway and back roads. Here is where I sold my special meat to the consumers, the other sinners. How this brought me joy as I watched the juices dribble down their chins! It was pure gratification as I saw their throats swallow. Metaphorically, this was my sex and I was in climax instantly. When the days arrived that I couldn't continue to be mobile, I would set the stand up in front of my new home. The gas station was rundown and only one room of the hotel was in working order, but this did not bother me. You might tell yourself that this is a dumb idea, to do this at my offering place, my holy house, but I never got caught. Sometimes an officer would come by, but never see me. I continued to liberate and cook as many as I could. This escalated into the year until a sinner walked into my perfect immaculate world. The stove was ready, but so was she. I felt a connection, but the cook can't teach the meat how to die. Only show them.

8.

The sisters remained silent after discussing the past. Julie knew her sister had been conflicted about the teacher who almost molested her. The teacher, Mr. Neal, had grown a long garden of awkward stares and sexual innuendo. He had been tutoring Katie for geometry and finally after weeks of gazing and gracious compliments, he took full action. In his mind it was time to water the garden. His advances had been firm at first. Katie admitted that he asked for sex, but she turned him down. That's when the water from his garden hose erupted and fast. The fact that insertion hadn't happened was quite surprising. Katie could feel him almost inside, when suddenly something within her gave her strength. A rush of fury collided within her. She bit at his neck, almost puncturing his jugular. Then, in that tiny window of opportunity, she struck with vengeance and clawed out one of his eyes. She took her bloody hands to his throat, and strangled him, until she realized it would be murder. She stopped and fled his house. Julie had always been mesmerized by the story and wished in reality that she could tell Kyle to get lost.

Now they drove, alone in their thoughts as metal music clamored in the small car. Kyle was undisturbed by Disturbed and kept chasing the Sandman. Julie's stomach rumbled and her whole body trembled with the tremor. Her sister even heard the growl over the music. Katie looked over at her.

"Was that your stomach?"

"Yes, I told you I'm starving," she replied. Katie laughed and turned her attention back on the road. About sixty feet in front of them was a big brown rotting sign. It read *Burger N' Beef stand.* Julie pointed, without saying a word.

"I don't know. We're in the middle of nowhere. Isn't this how bad things usually start?"

“Well, I’m hungry and it’s on the way. Besides Kyle’s out like a light. Maybe they’ll have a signal or someone can help with the tire,” said Julie. They passed the sign. Julie thought it over in her mind. They were approaching a small abandoned gas station nestled in front of a rundown motel. A sun-beaten wood sign, with fading writing spelled BEEF. Julie steered the Camry in the direction of the stand. She turned off the song *“Down with the Sickness”* and slowed the car. Katie turned in her seat and pinched Kyle’s knee. He shot up and cursed severely. He glared at his girlfriend.

“Time for a break,” she said.

Kyle stepped out of the Toyota and squinted. The sun was bright as it brought clarity to his eyes. The desert dust billowed as a small wind crept up. Across the reservation, from behind the deteriorating building, came a putrid smell. Katie coughed a little. She cleared her throat.

“I don’t like this,” she said. In front of the trio, the gas pumps were decomposing; their hoses were long destroyed. The awning above them had holes and a murder of crows cawed.

Abruptly, they flew up into the hot air and into the bright sky. Directly behind the two gas pumps, sat the rotting building. Its glass windows were smashed and shattered in different spots. A few walls had crumbled and a Gila Monster raced out from the broken foundation. Off to the left of the station was a tiny motel with six rooms. The walls used to be orange, but were now sun rotted and burnt. Their exterior had been colored with graffiti multiple times.

“Looks deserted,” said Kyle.

“If that’s the smell of the food, I change my mind. I don’t want any,” said Julie as she squatted to look at the damaged tire. “Wow, we did a number. Now the tires completely flat.”

"Well, maybe somebody can help?" replied Katie, as she started for the front door of the gas station.

"Wait!" said Kyle, "I don't see any smoke from any beef stand. Nobody's cooking a thing!"

She turned to look his way and saw his eyes staring at her sister who was still squatting. Her purple G-string was hanging out and so was most of her behind. The tattoo of a jellyfish was inked on one of her cheeks.

"Kyle!" shouted Katie. Kyle jumped as if someone had placed dynamite under his feet.

"What?" he asked.

"I saw you. Now are you going to be a man and go inside? Or should I harness my strap-on?"

"Look, no one's here. Let's walk around and have some fun," he smiled. Julie was now beside her sister trying to peer into the station. The whole building looked vacant.

"Hello!" Julie shouted, but no person returned her yell. She pulled her phone from her pocket; it still had no signal. Katie looked at her sister in wonder. Julie just shook her head. Kyle removed his from his pocket, "Same thing," he said. Katie looked down at hers. "Ditto."

Julie could feel her stomach tremor as if her intestines were a fault line. She also had stored her bladder up like a camel's hump. She began a hasty walk towards the front door. Its glass was only shattered in one spot. There was no chain. When she yanked on it, the door opened quickly; without conflict.

"I'm going inside to use the bathroom. Do whatever you guys want to." She walked inside the broken building.

"Hold up, I'll go with you," shouted Kyle. He looked at his girlfriend. He could tell by her face she was mad. Before entering the fractured building, he said, "To protect her, like you said -got to be the man right?" Before Katie could answer, he left her outside in the suffocating sun. She was about to march in and kick his ass, when she thought she saw movement over by the motel. She noticed a door was open that wasn't before. *Screw them,* she thought, *after all this is done, Kyle and I are finished. I'm moving away from both of them.* She trekked across the hot surface of what once used to be a parking lot. Crumbled asphalt crunched under her sneakers. Ants tried to scurry away before being smashed. The group had split up, but she was tired of them anyway. Her suspicions of Kyle now seemed clear; if only her sister could or would confirm it. She wiped at her forehead; sweat was racing down like an avalanche. As she advanced closer to the motel, Katie couldn't help but feel watched. It was a feeling of nervousness that crept up her spine. It sent tingles throughout her body from head to toe. Before her, the motel rooms looked battered and beaten. Decades of weather had kept eroding the building day by day. Her feet came to rest on the broken concrete that was once a walkway. It resembled a porch, reminding her of old western movies. But her feeling of paranoia went deeper: this was her in a scary movie. One of those horror films that Julie loved, but she hated. Surely no one could be here. But still the door of the room marked 1, taunted her as it stood ajar. She cupped her hands around her mouth.

"Hello?" she yelled, but the words just echoed around her. No answer came. No reply from either man or animal. She continued to walk up to the door and then she disappeared behind it.

Inside, room number 1 was clammy, and foreboding. The room should have been disgusting, but instead someone had remodeled the entire room. The floor should have been rotting out due to mold and weather, but no floor was present. Dirt covered the entire space. The walls looked as if fresh paint had been applied. Katie's fear elevated with her discovery. She tried the light switch. To her disappointment, no light shone from the ceiling fan. A mattress sat on the dirt to her left. The bed had been recently made and tidied. She went to the bathroom door and tried opening it. The lock had been set. She tried again, but it wouldn't budge. As a cloud moved away from the scorching sun, a small light entered the room from above. Katie looked up and saw a skylight had recently been added. The rays from the sun disclosed shelves on the walls around her. Weird sculptures had been carved out of some white material. She walked over to one and felt it. The texture was not wood or plastic; it was more solid, smoother. The whiteness reminded her of bones. But it couldn't be, could it? The sculptures were of small figurines which resembled people but none of the statues had appendages. It was all carved into one solid piece. Next to the shelf she was by, hung a crossbow with the bolts resting next to it. She remembered how she took archery, and arrows were for bows and bolts were for crossbows. Next to the bathroom door was a small circular table. Laying on top of it was a little pocket book. The coloring was black. She ran her fingers across the front; its cover was leather. It had been engraved with a D. Katie snatched up the book and proceeded to sit on the mattress. Against her better judgement, she decided to stay in the room. The feeling of being watched had subsided for now. Paranoia had taken a slight turn. Her interest now was the book. She opened the small paperback.

9.

The air was thick with dust as Julie entered the station. Her full attention was centered on finding a toilet. Sun rays shone down through decomposing holes in the ceiling. As her eyes adjusted to the light, she saw a door off to the left of her, with a bathroom logo on it. The shadows were hiding the real terrors that lay here. Even if the darkness wasn't camouflaging it, she would not have noticed the horrors around her. She made it to the door and swung it open hard, and screamed. Her scream was not of surprise or fear, but of anguish. No toilet sat inside the room and hadn't for a long time. The space was completely rotten. Suddenly a hand touched her shoulder. She turned and gasped.

"Don't do that Kyle!" she screamed.

"Sorry. Hey, no bathroom, that does suck."

"Yeah it does. Now come on, let's get out of here," she said as she headed for the front door.

"No, let's have some fun," said Kyle.

Julie stopped walking and turned to face him. Her anger was bursting at the seams. Her eyes dark with madness.

"Are you out of your damn mind? No way, no fucking way. You're sick!"

"You are going to suck me off right now, or I will tell Katie all about our affair."

"Katie is right outside; you're nuts!"

He grabbed her by the neck, forcing her to her knees. She wobbled slightly, but he remained holding her down. "Do it! Or I'll tell her all about us, and we'll see what kind of car ride we have for the next three hours!"

Julie glanced around the room. She felt watched and uncertain. There was some kind of presence here, she could feel it. They both were under the light from the decaying roof. In her heart she knew she would have to be the one to eventually tell Katie about the affair. Maybe if she ran, Kyle would not catch her. Then again if she told her sister now, he would deny everything she claimed. She figured if she did it this one last time, maybe her sister would catch them and then know the truth. She remained on her knees and unzipped his blue jeans. She opened her mouth. The lust had reached the highest point. Neither Kyle nor Julie saw the shadows release a form behind them. Out from the depths of the blackness came a man. Within his hand he held a wooden baseball bat. With one swift move he knocked Kyle in the back of his head with the bat. The blow wasn't hard enough to be fatal, but knocked him out cold. Julie tried to scream, but her voice was muffled as the bat came down onto her. She lay there unmoving, but breathing. The man smiled and whispered, "Sinner."

10.

Katie studied the words inside the small pocket book. They had been typed some years ago and apparently had to do with either a secret fraternity, or a secret organization centered on some sort of religion. The first page had a picture of a crow with the numbers 14:14. This is how it began:

This is the bible of death which has been passed down through the ages, both verbally and recorded. These words have been brought to life by the angels who serve our Lord swiftly and obediently. They brought the teachings in visions within rainbows and night time. It is by their lead that we accept our calling and follow them into battle.

Supreme Ruler and Beautiful Master of the universe! We love thee and succumb to thee. Please invoke thy blessings at this time. Clothe this candidate in harmony and magic of the night. Grant this candidate a true and faithful blessing. Purge this candidate of any falsehood that has constrained thy spirits.

Firstly, you shall shed all ideology, all possessions that bond you to this world. Secondly, you are now no longer human. To be human is to be the flesh of sin. You are sinless now. Thirdly, this is the law of our fathers and our forefathers. You will never disclose any subject of ours, or any information of our own kind to any human, unless it is for disciplining them and bringing them onto our side. Only lie with a homosapien if it is for creation. For most are born like us, only a few have ever become us. Candidate please repeat and sign these vows.

Do you declare, upon your honor and uninfluenced in any way possible, that you freely and voluntarily offer thyself to our order? To the mysteries of our universe?

After that sentence a handwritten name followed. It read *Michael D.* By now all that Katie had read perplexed her. It was fascinating. For this brief time she forgot all about her sister and Kyle. She continued reading.

Do you declare, upon your honor without hesitation or remorse, to carefully and cheerfully conform to all ancient establishments within this order?

Michael D.

Yes, behold how great and pleasant it is to be in the house of the Lord. We welcome you into our universal house of light and understanding. You are no longer human but a bearer of knowledge and a liberator of souls. Welcome, my brother into the house of The Arcane Dominion. May peace and pain follow thee. Katie took a breath and began to skim through the pages. As her eyes glanced upon the print, words that sprang up at her were, *fortitude, temperance, tools of liberation, and recipes.* As she got closer towards the back of the small book she saw handwritten stanzas. She slammed the book closed. She felt weird and naked. Something in those words felt so mystical, so hypnotizing. She had become thirsty and irritated. She headed outside. It was time to get the hell out of this spooky place.

11.

Katie Mears shielded her eyes with her right hand as she stood outside. The heat was unrelenting in midafternoon. As she squinted, she noticed a red Dodge pickup had parked a little further away from the gas pumps. It looked as if two people were sitting inside, but they didn't move. She couldn't tell if it was her sister and boyfriend. She made it to the gas station and peered once more towards the truck. She couldn't tell from the distance who they were, but the driver was not inside. As she traveled into the gas station, she noticed blood on the ground. She bent down to touch the substance and realized it was fresh. Frantically, she backed up and stumbled backwards, falling over and scrambling outside into the heat. Suddenly from the right of her, a male's voice spoke out, startling her.

"Hello, my name is Joey Dawson," the voice said. She turned to face the man. He was a solid figure, but short. His eyes shone kindness and his voice was calm and hypnotic. His hair was wavy and looked as if he had just gotten out of bed. A little stubble had been growing for a few days on his chin. He had to be in his late thirties. He wore a plaid flannel that was unbuttoned, with no undershirt. His legs held a pair of black jeans. Even though she was scared, Katie was instantly turned on for a moment.

"Hello Joey," she said. "Where do you come from?"

"From here," he replied and took two steps closer. "This is my property. Are you in some kind of trouble?"

"My tire's blown and I'm trying to find my sister and my boyfriend. Are they there, in that truck? Is that your truck?" Katie asked, taking one step back and then one forward. She was beginning to feel weird. But something about this man screamed *loveable, friendly*.

"No, they're not in there. You know, you're very beautiful. I can help you with the tire, but I want to show you something first. There's something about you that I like and I hope you would consider doing this with me."

"No, I've got to find my sister and boyfriend."

Joey lashed out at her. He gripped her throat and brought her to the ground. He began to strangle her. His grip was tight and fierce. His handsome face radiated with excitement as he continued to choke her.

"Don't make me kill you! I want to show you! I have to show you!" he screamed.

But even as she heard him say this, her eyes started to roll into the back of her skull. Her breath became slower and slower. She tried to raise her arms but this wasn't like the teacher Mr. Neal, this was something more sinister. This man had power she had not felt ever. As her vision went darker, she felt how soft his hands were. She began to enjoy it until all feeling stopped and her mind was no longer there.

12.

When consciousness and feeling came back to her, Katie opened her eyes. Daylight rained down upon her from the skylight. Her eyes recognized the interior of room 1. She tried moving her arms and realized she had been constrained. As feeling came back to her neck, she looked down and saw zip-ties holding her wrists together. Katie jerked her head around the room and saw Kyle naked on the bed, and bound together by zip-ties on his ankles and hands. His mouth had silver duct tape across it. A welt protruded on the side of his head. Julie wasn't anywhere in sight. She realized her mouth hadn't been muted, and that she was still clothed. She opened her mouth, "Julie!" she screamed. But no answer came. The door of room 1 flew open, startling Katie. Joey Dawson stepped over the threshold and stood before her. He looked agitated and angry. His shadow washed over her as she remained resting on the ground.

"I told you, I didn't want to have to do that. I need to show you something," he said. Joey still had on his flannel and black pants. What looked like blood marks claimed the lower portion of his unbuttoned shirt. He pulled out a cellphone from his back pocket. He fumbled with the front of the screen. It looked like an infant trying to figure out a toy.

"I feel like there is some sort of connection between us. Something only you and I would understand. A connection based on pain, but also of repression," he said. Katie remained quiet. She was studying him and was still trying to recover from her drowsiness. Joey continued to fiddle with the phone.

"I apologize Ms. Mears. I don't normally use these contraptions."

"How do you know my name?" she asked.

“I went through your purse and vehicle,” he stated. Finally, his finger stopped scrolling on the phone.

“Where’s Julie? Where is my sister?”

“All in due time, Katie. Now here, I want you to watch this video. I recorded it about two hours ago. If you wouldn’t have been asleep for so long, we could have gotten started a lot earlier.”

“Start what? Let me go! Let me go, you bastard!” Katie cried. Joey placed a hand on her head. He ran his fingers through her hair and down onto her cheek. The skin felt smooth and holy to him. He continued down, almost to her breasts. He hesitated there, and then rested his hand above them on her heart. Katie broke out in a small wave of tears.

“Are you going to kill me?” she asked. He grabbed her by the chin. His grasp was firm, rock solid. He smiled at her, he was very handsome.

“No, not if I don’t have to. Now please shut up and watch!” he thrusted the phone in her face. Obediently she stayed quiet and watched as the video started.

13.

Julie awoke in a shadowed room. The darkness climbed the walls and fought against the light streaming in through a shattered window. The ray of light revealed she was on tile and in a bathroom. Ironically, a toilet sat in front of her. Next to the toilet was a bathtub. A putrid smell rose up into her senses. She tried to cough, but only gagged due to the tape spread across her mouth. The smell was deep and foul. She scanned the area and noticed her leg had been shackled to a pipe. Her hands were zip-tied and her wrists bled a little. The chain around her ankle had been locked to the pipe. The rod protruded out of the ground which looked rotten and unstable. Trying not to panic, she slowed her breathing. As quietness crept into her; she heard a murmur from outside the door. Her eyes drifted back to the pipe. She jerked her leg hard. The rotten thing broke free from the smashed tile and flew into the tub, along with the chain. Julie realized she was naked.

She bent forward as far as possible, and brought her free foot to her mouth. Using her toes she was able to snag a corner of the tape and rip it off her mouth. She almost screamed, but realized that no salvation was here. Her best hero would be herself and the element of surprise. Julie stood to her feet, heading for the door when she fell down. The chain was lodged in the bathtub. Something in the tub was holding her. Once again she jerked as hard as she could. Into the air the chain sailed. Followed by drops of blood and a *ribcage*. The ribs fell to the tile in a horrid splintering sound. The rain of blood splashed around it. Julie covered her mouth as she peered over the top of the bathtub. Inside, smothered in burgundy blood were body parts and bone pieces. Legs, arms and feet had been tossed in. A human head with a spinal cord looked hauntingly back at her. There were two dismembered bodies resting, wearing their insides. The blood was synonymous with the water, mingling in its depths. Instead of a scream, she vomited. And then hurled again.

14.

Katie Mears watched in silent anger as the video played before her. Somehow this man named Joey, had recorded Julie giving Kyle oral sex in the gas station. Her eyes began to fill with water until the dam broke, spilling down her cheeks. She glanced at

Kyle who could hear the sounds resonating from the cellphone. He shook his head; either trying to say no, or indicating disbelief. Katie did not care which; she was furious. But that didn't matter now. She calmed her crying. She glanced away from the phone and looked up at Joey, his brown eyes sparkled. He finally dropped the phone onto the bed next to Kyle. Katie stopped crying altogether and let out a sigh.

"Where's my sister?" she asked. Joey shook his head and grabbed Katie from underneath her armpits. He stood her to her feet.

"First, we handle this sinner. You see I come from a place of pain. A slow torture of agony that placed a fire in my soul. I also believe that you too, come from this place."

"I'm from Utah."

"No, your body language speaks differently. Will you partake in Kyle's releasement into salvation?" He pulled Katie along, until they were both standing before Kyle. As the duo stood in front of him, Kyle began to cry.

"Please, don't cry. You haven't even felt your salvation yet," said Joey, as he produced a shiny butcher knife from behind his back. The steel shined brightly as the sunlight hit it. Kyle sobbed harder. His blue eyes fogged with sorrow. His whole body trembled. His face flushed.

"Now, Katie, it is time to release this sinner to the Supreme Ruler. Into life he came naked and so shall he go naked. May he not be judged by appearance, but by his atrocities," said Joey, as he slid his hand and the butt end of the knife into Katie's right hand. Now both of them held the knife together at the same time. Katie whimpered and cried.

"No. Please, God," she whispered.

But Joey and God did not care. In a single movement of power, the sharp utensil sliced through Kyle's neck. The blood sprayed out onto Katie's fingers as both she and Joey finished the kill.

15.

Abraham Hicks approached the abandoned gas station. He had done this once a month, for as long as he could remember. He slowed his patrol car to a stop. What his gaze rested upon brought confusion into his mind. A Camry was there, with a blown out tire. All four doors were hanging open. The red pickup wasn't parked in its normal spot. Someone was here. He turned off his engine and stepped out into the dry desert. The badge on his chest sparkled like a jewel as the radiant sun penetrated it. He walked hastily, but with caution. He looked inside the truck. Blood was smeared on the passenger seat, and it was fresh, recent.

He turned towards the gas station door. He went inside and immediately took the flashlight from his belt. He raised it so he could see. As the beam traveled across the depths of the retired business, his eyes beheld ghastly terror. Hanging from hooks and plastered over the windows was human skin. Hicks could tell because some of the female anatomy was present, such as breasts. One woman had been draped across the window, her stomach had a tattoo that read Aries, signifying her star sign. The hides of the people had been stitched up and sewn across the station as if it were wall paper.

The smell climbed up into his nostrils and he coughed a little. A few bars of light came through the crumbling roof. Resting in these gloomy sun pools was more blood. A multitude of different sized saws, rested on top of the shattered counter where the register was. Two rotting bodies had been completely gutted and were now hanging from the roof by meat hooks. He studied them and realized the blood on the floor wasn't theirs. Their bodies were old and the wounds on them were dry. In fact on certain areas of their skin, there was mold. He noticed other tools lying in the far corner, which had to be from a butcher shop or meat plant. Abraham put his arm to his mouth and scrambled outside, trying to forget the horrible pictures that now slithered around in his mind.

16.

Katie took a few steps away from Joey, but he grabbed her and held her tight. His body odor rose from underneath his clothing causing Katie to forget all about how handsome he was. Kyle's blood trickled down from Joey's hands and onto his forearms. Katie could feel the same blood drying onto her fingers. Joey held her close and whispered, "You see, it's easy. The sinner must be punished. It is the way of our Lord."

"This is madness," said Katie as she struggled. "Let me go!" But her pleas would not work on Joey. He squeezed tighter. Both he and Katie still held the knife together.

"Would you like to learn how to separate the flesh from the wicked?" he asked, smiling.

Suddenly, the bathroom door burst open. In a stumbling manner Julie appeared from the doorway. Her eyes were wide with horror, but softened to relief when she saw her sister. Katie screamed and turned the knife outward, stabbing Joey in the upper portion of his thigh. It wasn't a crucial stab, but he let go of her body. She shoved him hard to the ground. The absent floor whirled up dust as he fell. Katie ran, reaching for her sister's hand. Julie grasped it, squeezing tighter than a python. Out from room 1 they raced. The heat struck Julie's naked body as she slowed her movement. She was panicking and her eyes were running like a leaky faucet.

"Julie, come on! Fucking move it!" Katie exclaimed. "We don't have time!"

Joey recovered from the blow he had received. He looked down at his leg. The knife was stuck into his thigh, deep. It wasn't fatal, however, and he smiled. The sheep always acted up once in a while. He felt saddened to know he would have to kill both of them now. He would take his time with Julie, and then make Katie eat her remains. The sinners always looked so beautiful on the stove. He scrambled to his feet and snatched his crossbow off the wall and grabbed the bolts next to it. Quickly, he made it outside and saw the two girls weren't far. In fact Julie had stopped altogether. He stuck his foot in the stirrup and pulled back the cable, cocking the bow. He placed one bolt into the loading chamber. Raising his weapon he saw the tiny red dot on the back of Julie Mears.

17.

Officer Abraham Hicks came around the side of the decaying motel. He saw two women. One naked and acting hysterical. A piece of chain and pipe trailed behind her from her ankle. The other woman was collected, but frantic none the less. The naked woman got closer to the other and they embraced. They used the sharp end of the pipe on the naked girl to cut their binds. He approached them carefully. The clothed lady saw him and now both women were rushing towards him. He pulled out his revolver.

"Stop!" he commanded.

"No! You don't understand! A man's here, he's trying to kill us!" screamed the clothed woman.

"Who are you?" Abraham asked.

"I'm Katie, this is my sister Julie. Please!"

The officer got closer to the sisters. Hicks looked at the naked female. He could see blood and sweat dazzling upon her body in the hot sun. Katie could see his gaze and looked him over. He had a tattoo on his forearm. In big black bulky ink, the numbers 14:14 were printed on his skin.

"You're one of them!" Katie screamed.

Then Julie winced in pain. She slowly looked down and saw an arrow sticking out of her stomach. The bolt had gone straight into the right lower side of her body. She stumbled forward towards Hicks. He kept his gun raised. But instead of rushing to Julie's aid, he said to Katie, "You need to go back inside."

Katie shook her head in disbelief. Her mind began to tumble as if all her thoughts were inside her stomach, sloshing around. She wanted to vomit. Vomit up all these feelings, all this *fear.* Hicks stepped closer to her, his full attention centered on her. Joey was still behind them, unmoving. This had never happened to him before. He studied the officer. Hicks grabbed Katie with his free hand. "Turn around and let Joey take you back inside. Our work needs to be completed."

Julie was bleeding out. Her senses were going in and out of her subconscious. She could hear what was transpiring. But her pain bloomed into her brain screaming for comfort. She crawled closer to the policeman. Without hesitating she opened her mouth and chomped down, closing her mouth around his ankle. Instantly, he wailed in pain, lowering the gun and releasing his grip on her sister. Katie went for the gun, she grabbed his wrist and twisted the weapon out of his grip. He wiggled his body trying to escape the clutches of Julie's mouth. He swung at Katie, but she ducked away from his blow. He swung again, punching Julie in the side of the face. Katie cocked the gun and fired. Then fired again. Julie met Hicks face to face on the ground. Two bullet holes were smoking from his face. One above his right brown eye, and half his mouth was gone from the other.

Joey Dawson rushed towards the group. Clouds of desert soared behind him as he sped across the sand. He was furious. He would deal with these sinners swiftly. No remorse was to be had for Katie. She did not understand. But she would, she must. A loud bang echoed into Joey's ears, and a sharp pain hit his shoulder. He stumbled backwards as another bang clanged. This time pain hit him a little lower than the previous shot. Another bang, and something grazed past his ear. *The bitch meat is shooting at me. She's actually shooting at a god!* He thought to himself, as he continued his charge. He was closer, and this time he almost saw the bullet coming as it entered his chest. He fell directly back in a beige cloud of dust. The scorching sun rained upon him as he stared up into it.

Katie knelt to her sister. The bolt was fully stuck into her stomach. The head of the bolt poked out from her front. She knew she had to pull the arrow out without breaking it in half. Blood pooled around Julie's stomach and lapped down her body in tides. The sun baked the substance onto her skin. Katie could feel this too, for Kyle's blood had become crusty on her fingers. She managed to get Julie to her feet and over to the truck. Katie swung open the passenger door for Julie.

“Here, I’ll help you in. Hurry!” cried Katie. Julie tried climbing into the vehicle, when something pulled her hair backwards and out of the truck. It was Joey. She tumbled to the desert ground. Once she was on the ground he tackled Katie to the floor straddling her. His movement was fast, and the crossbow and arrows escaped off of his shoulder and back. His solid smooth hands clasped Katie’s neck. He squeezed. As he did this he lifted her slightly, almost up to a sitting position and then slammed her body back towards the earth. The back of Katie’s head smacked the scorching desert and gashed open.

Out of her peripheral vision, Katie saw Julie motionless. Her sister did not move or make any sounds. This was going to be the end of the Mears. The sun penetrated the ground all around her and that’s when she saw the steel-tip bolts sparkle up towards her. They were within arm’s reach too. Slowly her fingers climbed the little hills of sand towards their salvation. She could feel her throat burning and crushing inward due to Joey’s strength. Her eyes began to fog. Finally, her fingers collected around one of the arrows and in a swift movement brought the steel tip directly into the side of Joey’s head. She could feel it pierce through his flesh and she pushed harder. The bolt gained space into his skull. Instantly, he fell off and away from her. Onto his back he landed and brought his hands to his head.

But then he lay there, unmoving. Katie leaped to her feet and raced over to her sister. She was breathing, but her face was as white as Casper. Katie picked her up and placed her in the pickup. Katie ran over to her car. Sure enough, all the doors were open and the insides of the vehicle had been vandalized. She saw her purse and contents scattered. She grabbed what she could and put it all back in her purse. She strung it over her shoulder and popped the trunk. She grabbed Julie’s things and hustled back to the truck. She threw all her possessions in and reached for the ignition.

Wait.

There was a problem.

No keys were inserted there.

Her sweat mixed with blood began to irritate her skin. She felt her body go numb. She thought of two possible solutions. Either the keys were in room 1, or they were on Joey's corpse. Her mind was screaming at her to rest. Her stomach was on the verge of exploding, and her legs complained. Still, she exited the truck and crouched before Joey's carcass. From the chest pocket of his flannel, a small keychain poked its way out. Slowly she reached for the keys. Suddenly, Joey's right hand sailed through the air meeting her wrist. His eyes shot open and he began to twist her hand backwards.

"No!" she screamed, and using her free hand; pushed the arrow deeper into his head. She pushed until it could go no further. He dropped her hand.

Now she was back in the truck. Frantic and sweating, she tried to compose herself. Terror was racing throughout her senses, speeding her heart into hard thumps. Finally she stomped her foot onto the accelerator. In a cloud of dust and bloody debris, she fled the beef stand from hell.

18.

The cemetery had a cool breeze rushing through it. The small blades of grass swayed in the wind as the clouds moved over and around the electrifying sun. Katie Mears was stationed on a plastic lawn chair. A hot coffee was in her hand. The steam rose from around the lid, sending the fragrance of grounds into the atmosphere. She sat in front of her sister's tombstone. It had been four weeks since the terrible day on the reservation. She had made it to the hospital, but it was too late. Julie passed away within the hour she arrived. The authorities took Katie's statement and went to Joey's gas station. Upon reaching the area, the police claimed to not have found any bodies, not even Kyle's. Katie realized she was on a fence. One side claimed to still be on the manhunt. The other side, the taller side, claimed that due to the accident with the Camry her sister had died in the crash, and that when Kyle went looking for help got lost and now is considered dead in the desert somewhere. Katie had a feeling that something was being covered up. But whenever she tried to start up the investigation or speak with authorities they all said the same thing, "We'll get back to you." She placed her coffee onto the damp grass and snatched a little black book that she had been reading, out of her purse.

When I saw her I knew she would be the one. I figured that I couldn't do this forever, even though all of me wants to. At first she would not comply, I had to strangle her to put her to sleep. She slept too long, but gave me enough time to get the two ladies out of my truck and into the tub. They are deceased now. I chained one sinner inside the bathroom. The other is on the bed. I wait patiently for them to awake. I will make the one called Katie sacrifice the sinner alongside me. This will be her first initiation, if it all goes accordingly. The stove is my home and their salvation. The stove is my life force. For within the fire, there is a cleansing. The perfect flame to cook my calling.

Katie closed the small book. She was fearful of showing it to the police. That one officer had been one of the members, or believers, or whatever it was they claimed to be. She stood to her feet and placed a pink rose on her sibling's grave. She left the chair and coffee in the cool grass. As she strolled through the place of death, where everyone was dying to get in, she cried. Her tears fell controlled, not chaotic, but with deep sadness. What was she going to do now? She reached the rental car she had obtained a few days ago. The yellow Kia Soul stood out like a sore thumb amongst the grey tombstones. She reached for her keys inside her purse when through the glass of her vehicle, she saw an envelope laying on the driver's seat. Her lips trembled and her legs shook. Just an hour ago she had locked all her doors and all windows had been rolled up. In fact the windows and locks still remained secure. She opened the yellow car, easing herself behind the wheel. She fondled the manila envelope in her hands. She peered out through her windshield. No one was around. Katie tore the envelope open and discovered a typed letter addressed to her.

19.

Good morning Ms. Mears. It is time we discuss the sadistic actions you took against our kind. As a whole, we appreciate the eradication of Joey Dawson. Both he and his father were becoming out of control. You see, within control there is order. We have a set of guidelines, or rules, that you now possess. It was very hard to clean up the mess you made. Your kind are so disorganized and sloppy. But we managed to keep a lid on the outcome. Sure, some information will leak, but we will handle that accordingly. It is with great servitude to the Supreme Ruler I write you. The Arcane Dominion lost one of its greatest in the defeat of Abraham Hicks. Now, you know about our great congregation. The time has come for you to either accept our peace offering; as you will become one of us. If you do not wish to learn our mysteries or our ways, then simply, you will die. We will break your body like bread and our stoves will flare with your flesh. Your blood will be drunk like our

Lord's is to be drunk. There is no other way. The only way is our way. Our path has many great leaders, many positions of power. Would you like to be in that power? Won't you take our cup of blood and become a legion? Our power stretches into and beyond that of your police force, leaders and government. Our hands are everywhere and so are our eyes. Tonight, or should I say tomorrow at 3am, you will receive another letter. That will be our final offering. Join, join our holy alliance or perish with the sinners. For you all look so beautiful on the stove.

Peace and pain,

The Arcane Dominion

Katie Mears dropped the letter. It floated peacefully downward, resting next to the brake pedal. She stared at her reflection in the rearview mirror. The world was a shadow place. A land filled with blackness and malice. Now her region had crumbled into sickness. Spiraling down a twisted staircase, never-ending. Spiraling, spiraling. The steps would creak with sorrow, all the days of her life.

The Stairs

...all the Earth was fire, which was the end of the First World...

-Hopi legend

1.

The smell of smoke congested Mr. Padilla's office. Clouds from the cigarette dangling in his mouth, floated up around his smooth black hair. His eyes were sharp, and full of anger. Owen Pratt was late again and his boss had a million sentences, filled with hateful words. The anger came spewing from his mouth, dodging the cigarette trembling in his lips. Owen stared at the tobacco stick. It was hypnotizing as it jiggled. Mr. Padilla removed the tobacco from his mouth with two bony fingers. He dipped the ash into the tray resting on his slender wooden desk.

"Owen, are you hearing me?" he asked. Startled out of his gaze, Owen nodded his head.

"Then, what's your job here?" he inquired.

"Dishwasher," answered Owen.

"If that's true, then why am I not seeing any clean dishes, or utensils before me? Wait! I know why, because you're late!"

"Mr. Padilla"- but his boss cut him off.

"How can dishes be clean, if you're late? Do dishes wash themselves, Owen?" questioned Mr. Padilla.

He continued to stare at his boss. Mr. Padilla glared right back.

"Speak, when you're being addressed, boy!"

"No sir, dishes can't wash themselves."

"Should the lovely waitresses wash dirty dishes? Should the cooks wash the dishes? Tell me, what their jobs are." He returned the tobacco to his lips and inhaled.

Owen sat staring coldly at Mr. Padilla. This man had been his Achilles heel for the past three months. He wiped his right hand across his sweating forehead. He knew he should answer, being silent never worked with the boss.

"They take orders from the customers, and the cook makes the food. He prepares it for the customer," answered Owen. His boss blew the smoke from his lungs.

"And what do I do?" he asked.

"You take the money and pay us," replied Owen.

"See, I knew there was some intelligence in you. Too bad though. You're fired!"

Owen tried his defense, "Mr. Padilla, it won't happen again."

"This was the eleventh time in three months! Goodbye Mr. Pratt."

Owen stood up and glared at his now former boss. He knew of all the dogs in the park, Mr. Padilla was the loudest. His bark and bite radius were synonymous. Sighing, he turned and exited the office. He left behind the fog of smoke choking the filing cabinets and the dog whose bark had just ended Owen's pay. He maneuvered around the maze of brown chairs and tables. Short Stack restaurant was a small hole in the wall breakfast joint. But they were renowned for their vast array of pancakes. He knew he would miss working here. He opened the door of the restaurant and was almost out, when a girl's voice cried to him.

"Owen, where are you going?"

It was Ali Polag. The girl he had been seeing for a month.

"Mr. Padilla just fired me," he said.

Ali Polag gazed deeply at Owen. His average build and deep green eyes made her smile. She had loved getting to know him the past month. He had on a black AC/DC shirt and jeans. His long curly brown hair flowed down resting on his shoulders. Just staring at him made her womanhood tremble. Her hazel eyes began to swell up. She wiped her hands on her apron. It was slow in the afternoon. She had already made her rounds at the tables.

"What an asshole," she said. She took steps toward him, her blonde pony bouncing as she came. He opened his arms, welcoming her embrace.

"I know," he said, "but what's done is done. Just got to keep moving on."

She had her head buried in his chest. Damn, he smelled wonderful. She wished she could bottle the scent up and take it home with her.

"Can I come over tonight and make dinner?" she asked.

"I don't know Ali. I have to see what Eric and Trish are doing."

"Your roommate is so fussy!"

"I know; he didn't use to be like that. Not until he got Trish moved in with us."

Alex Padilla stormed across his restaurant and into the foyer.

"Go home, Owen!" he ordered. Ali winked at Owen as he left his old job, and stepped outside into the warm New Mexico air.

2.

The hot air blew against his skin as he traveled down Gateway Ave. It was still afternoon in Gibson, New Mexico and he figured instead of taking the bus home, he would walk. Walking always took his mind off to different thoughts. He had moved here with his best friend Eric Silva. The two had been best friends since high school. But when a female enters the world of boys, they either become men or stay boys. Even in certain circumstances, they become manchilds. Owen figured that's what he was. He loved comic books and classic rock. He refused to cut his hair and would hit the bong occasionally. Four months ago his brother and father perished in a car accident. They had been walking back from the grocery store when a truck ran right over them. Owen's mother was devastated and he wanted to move back with her, but she refused him. Suddenly, his pocket began to ring. He pulled his cellphone out of his denim pocket.

"Hey Eric, what's up man?"

"Owen, I have something to tell you. I know you'd punch me, so I thought a phone call would be better," his friend said.

Owen stopped walking. He stood on the crumbling sidewalk. Two skateboarders rolled by. The wind picked up causing the desert willows to wave their leaves at Owen.

"What happened now?" he asked.

"Trish and I have been talking. We think its best if you moved out."

"You're fucking kidding me dude?"

"No, I already boxed your things and have them on the porch," replied Eric.

"What happened, man? I'm like your brother, I needed you and you were there for me. I'd do the same for you!" shouted Owen. He began walking again.

"Look, I'm still here. I'm just a little farther away. I really love Trish, man. It's just time to grow up. Think about the future."

"The future is never certain," said Owen, as he hung up on his friend. He looked up and saw his feet had taken him to a liquor store. Owen had thirty dollars in his wallet. Time to get boozed up. He strolled inside and nodded towards the clerk. The cashier returned the nod with a slight head pop. Nestled inside the glass cage underneath the register were the lottery tickets. The purple, blue, and red colors taunted Owen gleefully. He went up to the clerk. The two men stared at each other.

"Well, I was going to get as fucked up as possible. But instead I'll take thirty dollars in scratchers."

"Living dangerously, or stupidly?" asked the clerk, as the transaction was processed.

Owen ignored the man and hustled outside. He ran across the street to the bus stop and perched on the bench. Using his soon to be old house key, he scratched away at the cards. Nothing on the first one. Nothing on the second. The shavings whisked away on the wind, just like tiny ripples in time.

Owen was becoming agitated. In his heart he hoped this hadn't been a waste of money. He threw the bad cards into the street. The breeze picked them up and carried them down the roads of Gibson. Then a winning number appeared. He smiled a big pearly smile. His grin stretched from cheek to cheek. Another winning number surfaced. His luck was beginning to change. Onto the next card. He gripped the bright red card fiercely. His heart thumped faster. He was up to almost five hundred dollars. The next card was a dud. His happiness began to dwindle. But there were two cards left.

Yes! Another winning card.

He yelped in joy. The last card began to shake in his left hand as his right hand scratched its surface. His body became tense, almost like a rock. He was hardened with suspense. The last number emerged. It was big, impressive. It read jackpot. One-hundred-fifty-thousand dollars were now his. His heartstrings tightened with new found energy. Now he could help his mother, and for a while, be carefree. The squealing brakes of the old blue bus clamored. He stashed the winning cards into his pocket. He grinned all the way up the steps, and did not stop smiling once seated.

Everything was going to be okay now. This new door had opened for him. Luck had grabbed him by the hand, pulling him in the direction of dreams. That was all any of us really have. Dreams that stew in our heads, boiling. Dreams that we promise ourselves to execute. Dreams that torment us. Dreams that are only real, when the Sandman visits. Dreams which burn out, and fade away. Owen gazed out the window at the dreamers passing on the sidewalk, knowing they had to be asleep to believe them.

3.

It was two weeks later in May. Owen had bought a house on the outskirts of Gibson. The surrounding area was flat and overflowing with fields. Owen didn't mind the grind of the tractors. The noises of the day here, were like lullabies compared to the bustle of the city. An orchestra of crickets was the cacophony every night and that didn't bother him either. The house was a three bedroom abode with slender hallways. The kitchen was petite, but bedrooms were fairly portioned. The home sat on an acre which delighted Owen. However, the brown exterior was bothering him. He now sat on the porch in a wicker rocker with a Bud in his hand. The beer was his third one in about forty-five minutes. He glanced over at his neighbor's house. The home sat thirty yards away. A crazy old Indian woman lived there. The realtor mentioned that she was of Pueblo and Hopi descent. The realtor told him to keep his distance though, that the previous owners had ran into a lot of trouble with her. Upon asking the whereabouts of the old owners, the realtor refused to answer. Owen drank his beer, listening to the birds in the big Bur Oak shadowing his home.

Out across his pebbled driveway, a roadrunner sped. His sleek narrow body raced over the tiny rocks. His scrawny legs tossing up dust, just like in the cartoon. Owen's gaze followed the bird until loud honks disturbed him from his stare. His mother was pulling up in a magenta Dodge Neon. The little car looked humorous out here in the wilderness. The car came to a halt shortly behind Owen's new Tacoma. He could see the backseat was filled with suitcases and clutter all the way to the ceiling. His mother, Linda, removed herself from the car and waved. She had been excited to come live with her son. Owen shimmied down the steps and walked over to his mom. They embraced.

"You're drunk already?" she asked. Owen smiled and opened the back door. A wave of suitcases poured out. They piled up before him almost to his knees.

"Don't worry, there's more in the trunk," she said.

Owen started helping his mother. The suitcases and boxes, continued to tumble out of her vehicle. His mouth was watering for another beer. Pausing from helping Linda, Owen climbed the porch steps. He dropped his hand into the ice chest. The water sent goosebumps up his wrist.

"Grab me one of those, will ya?" Linda said, standing in the doorway. Owen tossed one into the air. His mother caught it perfectly. They cracked them open and saluted together. As Owen knocked his back, he let his eyes wander. He brought his head back down and noticed his Indian neighbor staring coldly at them. Owen raised his can in the air. The old lady shook her head in disgust, and snapped her blinds shut.

4.

Linda Pratt sat on an indigo couch, with the indigo pillows, in the alabaster living room. The room was so white that the blue furniture almost resembled waves splashing in a surf. The oval spinning fan on the ceiling propelled the light washing over the tide. She had her head stuck in a Koontz novel. Her attention was so focused on the author's words, that when the power broke, she jumped about a foot off the couch fumbling the book. The story escaped her hands and plopped onto the cerulean carpet. Linda was consumed in total blackness. There was no light from the window behind her, night was here. Carefully, she began to shuffle across the living room space. Something sounded different. The crickets were not playing Fur Elise and all was calm. Then a steady noise floated out to her, a slow rhythmic sound. When her brain recognized the sound, she froze.

The sound was breathing. And it wasn't coming from Linda's lungs.

She sweated frantically. The breathing bore no characteristic of an animal. Linda knew there was another presence in the room. She wanted to speak, but the words stuck in her mouth and refused to be spoken. Her legs trembled slightly. Suddenly, the power regained. Standing before Linda was the woman from next door. Long black hair curled into two buns were stationed on the sides of her head. A headband of opals sat between them. Her skin was wrinkly and brown. It was aged with dark sun spots and Linda could almost feel the leather it resembled. Her torso was clothed in a dusty dirty manta. Her legs were bare except for the moccasins on her feet. The women stared at one another.

"Get the hell out!" cried Linda, breaking the silence. The neighbor did not leave. Instead, she waved her right hand, in a circular motion.

"They came long ago. We took too much, which is why their waists are so skinny. The fire and ice came."

"What are you talking about?" asked Linda. The Indian continued to wave her hand.

"They helped us in our peril. The help was needed for my ancestors' survival."

Linda took a few steps closer to the woman.

"Get the fuck out of my house!" yelled Linda.

The neighbor ran towards the front door. She stopped. She held her hand on the doorknob. She turned to face Linda.

"Do not go into the ground," she said. "They wait there. Sotuknang will become angry. They have waited many moons."

With the last word being said, the old neighbor vanished out into the night.

5.

Completely bewildered by the intrusion of her home, Linda scrambled into the kitchen. She saw her phone charging on the countertop. With a shaking hand, she dialed Owen. Of course there was no answer. He was at the movies with Ali. She stuck the phone into the pocket of her sleep pants. Linda busied herself from door to window, making sure they were all locked. How could that kooky lady have gotten in? Deep within her abdomen her bowels moved. After checking that all points of entry were secure, she hobbled over to the bathroom.

Once inside and on the most sacred of all thrones, she finally relaxed. The pearly tiles sparkled in a jubilant manner beneath her feet. The walls stood grounded in a ghostly grey. Slowly her heartbeat began to calm from the intrusion earlier. She hunched on the porcelain toilet waiting to be relieved. Then something felt wrong. A tingly pain invaded her nether regions. The pain was sharp, almost that of a sting. Something small, yet possibly hard, had entered her rectum. A burning exploded in her stomach. She tried to stand but all her efforts failed her. The mighty white throne held her and so did this excruciating pain.

Something was inside of her. Out from the depths of the endless pipes of plumbing something had emerged. Now in her stomach she could feel it climbing. Climbing her insides wanting to be free. Beneath her skin something crawled, the stinging rose again. This time the pain was everywhere. She felt it in her chest. Whatever it was, it felt like a multitude. Her body began to shake and contort as she rested on the toilet. Then her last breath came. Her pocket lit up from underneath the green plaid. The tiny fabric hairs concealed the cellphone as it rang.

And it rang, and it rang. There was no one home now. Only pain.

6.

Owen and Ali pulled up to the house an hour later. Ali was in great spirits. The movie had been amazing. She never thought she would ever see Star Wars on the big screen again, but number seven somehow managed its way into Hollywood. Owen despised much of what he had just watched. But the wine at dinner had been extraordinary. With their hands interlocked the young people entered the home. Ali was humming John William's score.

"Mom, I'm back. I tried calling you!" Owen shouted. But no reply came. Ali headed for the bathroom down the long oceanic hallway. Its thin walls encompassed her head and she felt like she was in a wave. She thought about life on Hoth, until she got to the door. It was closed. Strange; as long as she had known the Pratts they always kept it open.

She knocked on the door. But her thuds returned no sound. No answer came from the bathrooms interior. A cold, disturbing feeling pulsed into her. She felt worried and scared. Slowly, she opened the door of the bathroom. Slowly her eyes adjusted to the horror before her. Abruptly, she screamed.

Owen came flying down the hallway of blue haze and almost collided with Ali. Her body was shaking and her mouth trembled. Long streams of tears rained down her cheeks.

"What is it? What is it?" Owen pleaded. She took a unsteady hand to his chin and turned his head towards his mother on the toilet. He yelled and rushed into the ivory bathroom. He hovered over his mother.

"Mom? Mom?" he pushed her slightly. She did not move or speak. Her skin was very cold. Her epidermis pale like a ghost. Suddenly, her jaw drooped. Out of the opening came hundreds of *ants.* The small insects spilled out onto her chin, and formed a line down her neck, onto her chest and stomach. Their small copper bodies overtook her, as if a whole colony had taken refuge in the deceased woman. The ants paraded onto the tile and scurried straight for Ali. She stomped on them. She ran to Owen's side. Holding him in her arms, she tried to comfort him. Owen raised his hands to his face. Tears of sorrow and agony drained from his eye sockets.

7.

That night the crickets chirped a dirge melody of gloom. The darkness that consumed the land, now intruded into Owen's heart. His mother had known that he loved her, but what she didn't know was that the house was going to be hers. Now she was gone, never to be hugged or cherished again. Lost somewhere between hurt and the memories of time. Yes, Owen knew that time would heal the grief, the pain. He also knew that the memories would continue to sparkle in his mind's eye like diamonds.

Now next to Ali he slept. The crying had subsided as she had held him all night. It was deep past the midnight hours as they snuggled and danced with their dreams. Owen felt a tingly sensation on his legs. The feeling flocked up to his chest and shoulders. It felt as if his skin was burning, possibly stinging like a flame was pressed against it. Immediately he tore off the blankets that were across him and peered down at himself. He found thousands of ants biting him. The tiny tangerine bastards covered him from his toes all the way up to his neck. Their mandibles ripped into his boxer shorts. He winced and screamed in pain as they drove their tiny mouths into his flesh.

Then he opened his eyes.

He stared at his ceiling. Branches from the Bur Oak out front casted finger shadows across the room. He sat up on the king bed and got to his feet. Ali felt his presence move and mumbled, "Where are you going?"

"To piss."

The hall light shone like a moon over the blue paint in the hallway. It preserved a tranquil mood as it splashed against the walls. He arrived in front of the bathroom and hesitated. It still did not feel right to go in. Even after the police took statements and left, even after the paramedics and paperwork, even after all that had transpired in the previous five hours he knew he could not go in. He would pee outside. He turned around to leave and saw a small mound before him. It looked like someone had flung dirt onto the floor. He walked closer to the clump and watched as it opened up. Out of the orifice at the top, the ants sprang. They gushed out like a geyser. These ants were different from the ones that climbed out of his mother. They were the same ones from his dream; they swarmed together, forming a shape on the ground. The shape took the mold of an arrow, pointing towards the front door. This arrow of ants retreated in the direction they pointed.

8.

He felt his skin quiver. Tiny goosebumps surfaced on his arms and nape of his neck. He was both nervous and intrigued. How could that mound appear when he had just walked down the hallway not two minutes ago? He followed the insects. That was the only rational choice, even if it didn't seem sane. The ants scurried faster as he gained space upon them. As he left the hallway he spied another mound sitting in the middle of the living room. Another one sat in front of the door of his home. He paused, holding his foot in mid-air. In his mind he tried to discern if this was all another dream or actual reality. He saw the local paper resting on the coffee table. Without disturbing the mounds he switched on the overhead light. The mounds remained, and no ants rose from them. Owen snatched up the paper and peered down at the words. He realized he could read it just fine. The letters were not sporadic or jumbled. He was in the present, and he was awake. Then as if all this wasn't strange enough, his front door opened up into the night. The door had opened all on its own. The howl of the night air came roaring in. The arrow of ants moved again. It pressed onward and out over the threshold. Owen wasn't far behind.

The moon grinned a ghostly smile down from the heavens. Owen cursed when he saw a litter of mounds covering his front yard and driveway. A battalion of ants now drew together, forming an even thicker arrow. From the glow spraying out from his porch light, drilled onto the side of his home, he followed them around the side of his house. When the arrow of ants got to the backyard they *disappeared.* Owen stopped and dropped to his knees inspecting the ground. The little insects had vanished completely. The air blew against his sweaty skin, sending chills down his spine. He stood back up surveying his backyard and acre lot. One bright lamp had been assembled on the back of his home. It provided much light and a feeling of security. But now its miracle of light shone down onto an immense oval hole in Owen's backyard. He brought one hand to his mouth. He did not know if it was to hold back a scream or just because he was utterly shocked. There had never been a hole back here. The new addition to the yard was about eight feet wide. He walked up to it and peered over its rim. He tried to calm his nerves but they were racing around his body like an electrical current. He held both hands to the sides of his face and ran his fingers through his bed hair.

Down in front of his gaze were stairs. Stairs that led somewhere.

9.

These steps were not concrete or stone. They were solid dirt. The skin of the earth had been torn open and roots decorated the interior. Owen squatted and leaned forward over the pit. The stairs looked sturdy enough and there was just enough light left from the porch and moon that he could see it went deep. Without any weapons or Ali, he decided to descend the steps. His right naked foot supported his weight as he stepped. The soft soil filled the spaces between his toes. As he went deeper following the stairs, he noticed how the walls changed. They had become more clay like. After about thirty steps he rested. He could no longer see the top of the staircase. He realized how dark it had become. Then he felt a pain arise in his head. Right above his forehead. A swelling of pressure boiled between his eyebrows. He closed his eyes trying to bear the pain. When his eyes opened, the pain eased. But his sight had become different. He could see, but his vision had a third line of sight. He could see from higher up on his head, almost as if he had just sprouted a third eye. This new vision helped him see clearer in the dark. Tiny crystalized sand that had been absorbed and trapped the sunlight, now shone radiantly into this new eye. He continued down, hoping that where it led would be a place of treasures. He knew he should have gone to wake up Ali, but this was his house. He would take charge and find out how this hole got here. The deeper he went, the more a strange smell began to engulf him. It was a foul but sweet aroma. He coughed a little. The scent possessed his lungs and nostrils. Owen could almost taste it. The smell reminded him of coconut but it was too strong. Its rotten, bitter after-scent was nauseating. The air was cool against his shirtless chest. His leg hair spread apart, as goose pimples erected on his skin. Finally his feet halted on the last stair. He was now buried about forty feet underground. With his new eye he gazed upon a door that was closed before him. The door was wide and nursed together by clay and stone. Its structure was made up of sticks and grass. An elongated log had been locked across it. Graffitied onto the stone walls around it, were native carvings. Owen took a step closer, running his fingers across the etchings.

The drawings resembled people, but were not humanoid. They had square bodies and big bulgy eyes. The top of their heads had lines that looked like antennae. They wore Native American linen and some had been sketched holding hands with what seemed to be normal humans. Owen did not know anything of the Indian culture or what these symbols meant. But he knew he must see what was on the other side of the door. This discovery in his yard could be the find of a lifetime. He imagined himself on the cover of People or even the National Geographic. This was his property. He could charge tourists to come visit. Hastily, he lifted the log off its hooks. He dropped it to the ground. The timber door opened slightly and a sea of wind washed over Owen. Then a force pushed against him. He could not see it, but only felt it. Almost like an invisible hand was squashing him. He felt his body become tiny. He realized he was shrinking. Smaller he receded, smaller, smaller, until the door was like a skyscraper to him. And then he walked through, into the other side of the door, no longer his normal size.

10.

The subterranean lair was vast. The walls were composed of crystalized dirt. Just like before, his new third eye showed Owen that he was in a chamber. His skin was still dotted with goosebumps. The air was cool, but dry. Many corridors and tunnels had been constructed around him. The same putrid scent now saturated Owen's senses and he felt like vomiting. He heard a patter of feet. The sound echoed around him coming from all different directions. The scamper halted and he began to search the area in circles. Barely leaving the shadows, a colony of ants surrounded him. Owen became paralyzed with fear. His feet remained stapled into the ground, even though his mind said run. The insects remained calm; the only motion was their antennae striking the air, picking up Owen's vibrations. He realized he was trembling. He started to take deep breaths. He inhaled and exhaled slowly. Suddenly, out of the deep caverns, an ant rushed him. The insect paused, standing erect on four of its six legs. Its mandibles reached out around Owen's neck. But the bug did not choke or hurt him. Instead its antennae fumbled around Owen's body. The slender appendages combed over every inch of flesh. Behind this ant, materializing right before Owen, another creature appeared. It seemed humanoid. The body structure supported this claim, but its head was oblong, and black hollow eyes sat deep in its skull. The mouth opened horizontally, exposing pinchers. It shed its skin revealing all its arms and legs. The ant who was still holding Owen, released him and scrambled over the discarded flesh, past the new creature, and huddled in the shadows with his comrades.

"Do you know who I am?" asked the creature.

"I don't even know where I am," replied Owen, who was still stationed on his knees. "Or what the hell's going on? You killed my mother!"

"You are in the kingdom of the ants, and The Ant People. We had to kill her to bait you in; you opened our door."

"This is all just a dream; can I wake up now? What door?"

"The door you came through to greet me," the ant man said. His voice was deep like roaring thunder and Owen wanted it to stop. He got to his feet, his fear retreating.

"Fine, I'm leaving," stated Owen.

"Oh, you cannot leave, for you see, your kind were once guests in my kingdom. Many centuries ago, when the world was being judged, you were sent to my kingdom for safety. But you took us for granted. You ate all our food and degraded yourselves. When you were through with your women, you tried our women. When food ran out, you turned on us. But now the door has been opened, the tide is rising, and the Fourth World will be our domain."

Then without hesitation, the colony sprayed Owen with formic acid, and tore his limbs apart.

11.

Ali stood on the back porch screaming for Owen. But he never appeared, or answered her wails. With a flashlight, she searched the backyard. His Tacoma was still out front, so he had to be somewhere on the property. With the bright beam guiding her, she happened upon the eight foot hole. Above her, the sky was turning purple, day was awakening from slumber. Without thinking, she ran down the stairs. She took a breather. She had gone about fifty steps without stopping. She had to relax. If Owen was at the bottom of this staircase he was probably in peril and needed her help. Strength would be needed and she felt like she had already used about sixty-percent of hers. Her head started to hurt. A funny pain strained on her forehead. Her eyesight was changing. But she couldn't focus on it, Owen had to be down here. She hardly noticed the pain after a few more steps. Finally at the bottom, she gazed upon a large wooden door framed by clay and rock. She screamed a startled wail. Escaping out from behind the doorway, was an ant. But the insect's body mass was changing. As its body emerged farther out from the door, it grew. The insect became about the size of a Great Dane. Ali turned to flee, but the insect was too fast. Racing towards her, he spat a watery substance. The spray of acid washed the skin from her bones. She never made it to the first step.

The door creaked wider as more troops of ants pushed through. They were angry and ready. The day would be theirs to conquer. As the sun rose in the heavens, the humans' mornings would all lead to their final breaths. The army of ants climbed out into Gibson, New Mexico with eager malice. They went marching one by one.

Then two by two.

Then three by three, and four by four.

Then seven by seven, and eight by eight.

Nine by nine, and then ten by ten.

Later in the day of slaughter that left Gibson a ghost town, a little old Hopi lady of Pueblo descent hobbled across her lawn. Her frail body traveled into her neighbor's yard and into the back portion of the acre. She knew exactly where she was going. Into the hole and down the steps she went. She said a chant as she stood before the door. A rhyme that her kind knew too well. Slowly and with much frustration and burden, she placed the log back across the door. She latched it into place. But Gibson was the ants' garden now. A garden of blood and death. The flowers would bloom only with folly. Somewhere on the planet another door was being locked. And another being opened.

And the ants go marching one by one...

Garden of Flies

If all mankind were to disappear, the world would regenerate back to the rich state of equilibrium that existed ten thousand years ago. If insects were to vanish, the environment would collapse into chaos. – E. O. Wilson

1.

The garden is blooming radiantly; the creatures of the domain live as if their presence will never cease. They go out into the day, believing in their established order. The roaches all live in a colony; the beetles and caterpillars all live on the north side. The crickets and worms dwell on the west, and the rest of the world lives in the east. Their world is all built around allegiance to the ideals created by the roach. Their world is thought of as harmonious, even if one side lives more prosperous than the other. They always say that all bugs are created equal, but it never feels that way.

One day the beetle asked his mother, "Why is the cricket putting those signs in his yard?" His mother stopped eating the lettuce and replied, "He thinks a cricket will be a better leader than the roach. Even though the roach has provided us all with this bounty of lettuce, and garden we call home."

Confused, the little beetle tilted his head, "But aren't we all bugs?"

"Yes, but this is the way of our domain and so shall it be," she answered.

"It shouldn't be. I am the master of my own life. I should be able to freely"-

Suddenly, the ground shook so violently, that the mother beetle slipped off the lettuce leaf. Her son cried in surprise as he also fell from the foliage. A huge leg came out of the sky, crashing down around them.

"It's the Sky God!" cried his mother. She tried to shove her son away from their plant, but it was too late. A green fog was billowing towards them. The cloud of pesticide consumed them. Their trachea exploded inside their bodies. The life had been purged instantly. After the dust settled and the chemicals dissipated, a swarm of flies began to feed on the carcasses.

The beetle's brother, who had been fighting a war over in the east fields, arrived back to his home garden and lettuce leaf. The war had given him many travels and a sense of pride. But now it all crumbled at the sight of his home. He was angered and saddened to see that his family had perished. He crawled quickly over to the fly, who was feeding on his brother.

"Why?" he asked of the fly.

"There is no why and the answer is simple: This is the only life I know," remarked the fly, with a mouth full of juices. Just before the brother could respond to the fly, another lime green haze swept over the garden. The area reeked of death and genocide. Before he succumbed to the poison, the brother beetle realized we are all living in a paradox. There is no solace, no progress, this way. We must not let the world possess us, but we must possess the world. Live the life you have been given, and choose which garden to dwell in. Each garden has its harvest and the thrill of what is to come.

The Dress

When an impure spirit departs a person, it goes through arid places seeking rest and does not find it. Then it says ‘I will return to the house I left.’ – Luke 11:24

1.

He sat in his Hawaiian shorts, in his wheelchair, staring. The lime color clashed with the orange thread on his waist. His Caucasian body was hunched, dotted with epidermis spots. His shirtless chest spared Edward Beard no modesty to his boss's aging body. He started to speak. As his words left his mouth, they were raspy but sharp, "What is it you wanted to talk with me about, Edward?"

They were sitting in Ralph Goodwall's office. Ralph was ninety years old and his antique store, Marty's (named after his dog) had been standing on Twenty-fifth Place, for more than thirty years. Edward had only been working here for a year. He straightened his posture in the leather seat with the decaying armrests.

"Well, Ralph, a dress came in today. The donor was a jittery hoot, probably a little younger than you. Anyway, it's my anniversary tonight and I want it for my wife. Was wondering if I could buy it?"

Mr. Goodwall puckered his lips and then swished them side to side. His caretaker stood behind him. His name was Landon. Occasionally, he and Edward would play pool on the weekends. He was also a retired minister. "It's a beautiful dress," said Landon, indicating the garment resting on Edward's lap. The peplum dress was midnight black, with pink floral motif. "The man who brought it in, said its era was from the 1940s to early 1950s," said Landon.

"How long have you and your wife been together?" Ralph asked.

"Twelve years. She loves this vintage stuff," replied Edward.

"Twelve dollars, then," said Ralph.

"Thank you, sir."

The men shook hands. Edward left Mr. Goodwall's office and stepped back into the store. The place looked like a hurricane had hit it. Antiques ranging from chests, to china sets and clothing, covered the left side. The walls sagged with different shelves of vinyl's and figurines from Mickey Mouse to The Wizard of Oz. Old board games littered the floor on the right, along with towers of books and magazines. The smell was stale and hot. Edward walked across the desert of memory. He waved to his fellow employee Matthew.

"Got it for her, Matt," Edward said, reaching the clerk.

"Excellent. How much am I ringing up?" he asked.

"Twelve bucks."

"Sharon's going to love this," Matt said, as he bagged the item.

2.

After the transaction was done, Matthew waved and nodded as Edward left the store. He walked into the setting sun of St. Augustine Florida. As all summers went in Florida, the temperature outside was moist. A polarizing wave of humidity saturated him by the time he got to the bus stop. While waiting on the bench, he held onto his new possession tightly. He was eager to give the present to his wife. She loved everything vintage; she did not really have an exact favorite era, but loved all styles from the past. This love had rubbed off on him and he enjoyed working at the antique store. Sometimes such as today, a golden prize would arrive. With squealing brakes, the large bus clamored to a stop. As he ascended the steps he pulled out his cellphone. He dialed his wife and once seated, waited for Sharon to answer. As the streets whirled by in a concrete mass, his wonderful wife answered, “Hello, honey.”

“Hey babe,” he replied, “get all done at the salon?”

“Yeah, this old lady’s color wouldn’t stay; had to fight with it for a bit. But I’m leaving now. You on your way home?”

“Yes, Sharon, and I have a surprise for you.”

“Can’t wait Edward. Love you. See you in about twenty then,” said Sharon.

“Love you too.”

Sharon Beard left her beauty salon and plopped down into her Ford Escort. She was filled with joy. She had a wonderful day and wonderful customers. Sure Mrs. Dill’s hair color had been a bitch, but other than that, all her appointments went smooth today. Hair styling and cutting had been her dream ever since Jr. High. She had many boxes in storage filled with Barbies, whose heads of hair had been redone. Now it was time for her wedding anniversary. She pulled out onto Orange Street and followed the veins of traffic. St Augustine was a verdant place. It wasn’t anything like the beach towns of the west coast. No, here you felt more relaxed a sense of tranquility had blanketed the city. There were always tourists and floods; she hated floods. The storms were the worst part. But the people were friendly and the history here vast. It had beautiful Spanish architecture and claimed to be the oldest city in the U.S. She couldn’t help but keep grinning as she sat at the stop light. Two men in a Mustang convertible gazed at her. They began to laugh. She fluffed her cherry hair and waved. The light changed and she left them. Tonight was going to be a great night. They were having dinner at Pizza Alley. Italian food was their favorite. Once there, she would give Edward his new wrist watch. Finally she pulled into her apartment complex and hurried out of her vehicle. She was anxious to see her husband. She hummed a melody as she climbed the stairs to the elevator. It took her to their floor. With haste, she rushed down the hallway to apartment 16. Tonight was going to be a great night indeed.

3.

The Beards' apartment was decorated in such a clash of eras that Father Time himself would be amused. Not necessarily abstract, but each room had its own era, its own setting. Edward was in the 1980's bathroom with the avocado wall paper and dreary green tub. Sharon stood in the 1960 kitchen. She pulled open the opalescent cabinet and poured herself a glass of water from the pearly, oval shaped fridge. Upon taking the glass away from her mouth and swallowing the water, she spied a box on the countertop. She heard Edward getting dressed in the other room.

"Hon, is this for me?" she called. He appeared in the tiny hallway buttoning his dress slacks. A foam of toothpaste bubbled around the toothbrush stationed in his mouth.

"Of course, babe," he mumbled, and returned to the sink in the bathroom. With shaky fingers she slipped the twine off the cardboard box. Gently, she pulled off the lid. The box contained a dress. It was a beautiful peplum dress. It was a satin black, with bright floral accent. She held it up to her body. It seemed like it would fit. She rushed into the bathroom, startling her husband. She pounced and gave him a huge wet kiss. He returned it with a French kiss. Sharon tore off her clothes and grabbed his hands.

"Take me," she said. Edward decided this was one way to work up an appetite.

Later, as the night had closed in around the city, the lovers made their way down St. George Street. Finding a parking spot was nerve wracking, but Edward managed to squeeze the tiny car between a jeep and a Prius. Edward gazed at his wife as she removed herself from the car. Her curly red hair flowed from her head. She was wearing the new dress and it clung to her body, like a baby Kangaroo in the pouch. Her figure danced erotically with her shadow. The lamppost washed over her, showering her in a heavenly beam. Edward smiled and pinched her on her buttocks. She playfully smacked him on the shoulder and the two interlocked arms.

"I love my dress," she said. "How do you like your watch?"

Edward outstretched his arm. "Love it!"

Joyfully, they pranced over the cobbled streets and past the many historical sights. Their love was on fire; nothing could stifle this burning. Or so they thought. The drive home was different. Edward was a little too drunk on wine, and Sharon was melancholy. Her posture was so stiff that it reminded Edward of a scarecrow. As the tiny car traveled down the even smaller streets, Edward was becoming worried. He tried holding his wife's hand, but she would not return the gesture. She seemed far away. She seemed unnatural.

"What is it, honey?" he asked.

"I'm fine," she responded.

4.

Edward lay in bed already counting sheep. Sharon was in the bathroom. Something did not feel right. Something inside of her felt dark, a disgusting black feeling of dread. She gazed upon her face and arms. They were pale; she looked very anemic. Her eyes were shallow. She unzipped the back of the dress and pulled. Her skin began to sting. The dress was stuck somehow onto her skin. She tried undressing and each time, like rubber, her skin stretched with the dress in a painful pull. Maybe she was very drunk or very sick. Either way, she figured she was exhausted and she left the bathroom. She plummeted onto the bed next to her snoozing husband. She had nothing but nightmares that night.

Sharon's salon was small and modest. She, another woman, and their boss were all the employees the owner could afford. Sharon stood out front, fighting with herself to go in. The new dress would not come off. Not last night, not this morning, seemed like not ever. She still felt sick to her stomach, but also strong, reserved. She was wondering if somehow she had been slipped drugs. Her boss, Mindy Caldwell, flung open the glass door.

"You're late, Mrs. Beard!" she hollered.

"Yes, Mindy; not feeling too well."

"That ain't dress code!" Mindy continued to scream.

"Well, I can't take it off because…"

"Save it! You have clients, hurry up and then go home!" Mindy commanded.

Sharon entered, placed her smock over the dress, and was now washing a little boy's hair. His hair was outrageously curly. It seemed as if he was born with clown hair. As her fingers massaged his scalp, something in her said to squeeze. Without hesitation, she gripped his head and started to compress his skull. The boy raised his hands up to grab at her wrists.

"You're hurting me!"

"No, I'm not," Sharon stated, and squeezed tighter, her nails almost digging into his scalp. She looked up in the mirror and saw her face had a dark grimace. The boy had tears rolling down his cheeks. She relinquished her grip and washed the shampoo out. They walked back to the chair.

"I'm sorry Tony, I didn't realize..."

"It's okay," Tony said hesitantly, "just don't cut me." But she did. She did twice. Once with the razor and once with the scissors. Cut a little piece of his ear clean off. Sharon dropped her tools. Tony was screaming and crying. His mother was yelling, and Sharon shoved her to the floor. Mindy tried to intervene, but Sharon fled the salon, leaving nothing but tears and blood behind.

5.

The drive home was a blur. She didn't even realize she arrived, until she was already running up the stairs. She took the steps two, three at a time. In the elevator she paced nervously. Edward would be home; it was his day off. But maybe he would be out and she could lock herself in her room without resistance. She stood outside of her apartment door breathing irregularly. Finally she went in. Edward was reading on the sofa. She startled him.

"Babe, you okay?" he asked. He rose from the sofa, but did not walk towards her. "You look ill."

"Don't want to talk about it." She rushed into the bedroom. She slammed the door. Edward hopped over the couch. He tried the doorknob. Locked.

"What the hell, Sharon?" he banged loudly on the door. She did not answer. He banged harder. But there was no response. Sharon ignored his raps. The pounding was hard, but something else had her attention. She stood in the adjacent bathroom peering at herself in the mirror above the sink. Behind her, a shadow moved and then a force took her. She shuddered as she felt a surge strike beneath her bones. Without knowing why, but feeling that she had to, she opened the drawer on the vanity and removed one of her razors. With the blade she dug and cut into the palm of her hand. The blood ran down onto her wrist and forearm. She cut into her other hand and then dipped her skinny index finger into the wound. With her crimson finger she started to draw on her mirror. She wrote a name. Over and across the mirror in bloody lettering was the name Agnes. Following the name she wrote: *is here.*

Edward retreated to the kitchen where he found his wallet. He removed his credit card and hustled back down the hallway. With sweat falling in pools off his body, he managed to wedge the card between the door jam and frame, opening the door. Their bedroom was quaint. The queen bed was bathed in purple with onyx sheets. The walls were cream and littered with antiques of their favorite bands and movies. Edward flew by his X-Files case and rounded the corner into the bathroom. He saw his wife bleeding on the tiled floor. She glared at him when he entered.

"What the hell is the matter with you?" he asked, stooping down next to his wife. He grabbed her hands and held them up to the light. "Why did you cut yourself?"

"I don't know; it happened so fast," she replied. He stood and saw the writing all over the mirror.

“Why the fuck did you draw all over the mirror?” he questioned, as he pulled out the peroxide bottle and band aids from behind the now blood-stained glass. Sharon started to cry.

“It told me to,” she replied between sobs. He finished doctoring her wounds. He put everything back into the cabinet behind the mirror. He rested beside his wife, who still remained on the floor.

“Who’s Agnes?” he asked. But his wife stayed mute. He stood and placed her arms around his body. He picked her up and carried her to the bed. He laid her down softly. They looked at each other for what seemed like hours to Edward. Her eyes did not sparkle. Instead they looked joyless and dismal. He sighed heavily and placed a hand on her leg.

“Babe, what is it?” he asked quietly. She turned her head slightly. The movement was very lethargic.

“I don’t feel right,” she responded. He rubbed her leg.

“Get some rest. I’ll clean the bathroom. Anything I can do for you? Or anything you need?”

But Sharon was quiet. She rolled over onto her side, ignoring her husband and turning her back to him. He walked into the bathroom. But he couldn’t see what she saw. His eyes did not uncover the figure resting beside his wife: a demon with grey skin and black flakey hair. Its eyes bulged, as if the rotting neck of the thing was being squeezed. The demon took a steady foul finger to its chapped lips. It was the gesture to stay quiet and Sharon obeyed.

Edward quickly cleaned off the mirror. He was frightened and agitated. Sharon had done something freaky, and not in the good way. She had acted strange all night after dinner and now the following day she cuts herself. While he finished his task he tried to remain calm, but he dropped the bottle of cleaner twice. He noticed his arms had goosebumps spreading across them. Their room and bathroom had become quite icy. He made a mental note of this and a note of the name, Agnes. Finally the last drop of blood was cleaned away. He returned to his wife. She was fast asleep and breathing deeply. He saw a bruise on her shoulder that wasn't there before. He left the bedroom to let her sleep. Whatever this calamity or sickness was, rest would be needed. He went to the sofa with his laptop. He pulled up Google and typed into the search bar, *Agnes of St. Augustine Florida.* Many articles appeared. As he scrolled he felt his tongue go limp and mouth become dry. He didn't want to digest what he was reading. What he was discovering. His eyes were mesmerized by the computer screen. It was horror after horror unfolding with each document.

6.

His body froze and posture tightened. There were numerous articles about a woman named Agnes Clementine. She had been a big deal in the sixties for child abduction and witchcraft. Apparently this Agnes was all that came up in the search engine, with those words. He tried a few others, but it all circled back to Agnes Clementine. Here is what the articles proclaimed:

It was the summer of '66 and children around St. Augustine had gone missing month after month. The kidnappings were spaced and never the same. On the twelfth day of June, a young-eight-year old boy escaped the clutches of his captor. He was smart enough to call the police from a payphone and a dispatch picked him off the street. He gave a detailed description of one Agnes Clementine, who had been substituting at schools and seen around playgrounds. A rumor had been circulating around town, of a woman doing strange dances in parks, and trying to get young women to practice magic.

Two days later, three officers arrived at the suspect's residence. Agnes was seized at her house, off the north end shore of St. Augustine. Inside police found cages with bone remains. Nine of these discoveries were children. Two live children were found in similar cages in the basement. Their names have been withheld. Of the three officers that entered, two apprehended her. Agnes had been very beautiful and the two policemen proceeded to rape her and kill her, for what she had done. Except for Officer Kavner. He testified at court about what the police did. He himself had not done the raping. But that he was their look out. He stated that as she was killed, she professed her love of Satan. She chanted weird words. Which later, a linguist confirmed as Latin. She had cursed her dress she was wearing at the time of the rape.

The article continued, but he could not keep reading. Edward took a weird inhale of air. It lumped in his throat. His eyes became wet with shock, and tears of fear began to slowly descend his cheeks. There was a photograph of Agnes Clementine. She indeed had been very beautiful. But what she wore caused tremors in Edward's stomach. In the photograph she was clothed in a dress. It resembled the same one his wife, Sharon, was currently wearing. A dark sinister mood draped its curtains over the apartment. He wanted to scream out, but remained staring into the screen. He desperately wanted to flee, but could not gain the courage to stand. Out in the atmosphere of the Beard's apartment, Edward's phone rang in a distinctive manner. Startled, he dropped his laptop. The crash awakened him from his stare. He stood, chewing on his nails as he rushed to his cellphone. Maybe someone up above was looking down on him. It seemed as if that could be true. The caller on the phone was Landon.

7.

Landon Woodard sat outside the morgue. The rain spit against his car in a disgusting wave. He sat in his Altima, waiting for Edward to answer. The night had become ripe with tragedy. It always seemed, on rainy days, that the deepest sorrows arise. As if the drops are mocking the situation and the thunder laughing back in a hollow boom.

"Hello?" Edward picked up.

"Hey, Edward. I'm sorry to have to tell you about Mr. Goodwall."

"What happened?"

"Mr. Goodwall passed away tonight. About an hour ago, maybe two. Just went to sleep," answered Landon. He turned on the wipers. He rubbed his stubble on his chin.

"Not Ralph," Edward said. "Where are you now Landon?"

"Right outside the morgue. Why?"

"I know you're retired, but something isn't right with Sharon." Edward replied. His vocal tone faltered. He breathed deeply into the line, causing Landon to hear nothing but static. Finally Edward continued.

"I think we may have something spiritual taking place in my apartment."

"Edward, what do you mean? What's happening?"

"Something not good. Something, wait, hold on," Edward put the phone down. There had been a noise. He looked up and saw Sharon standing, staring coldly at him. The tiny bulb above the couple encompassed them in a taunting glow. Her skin was turning pallid and her hair stringy, messy. Her eyes were glazed. The dress was almost pitch black and the flowers had lost their coloring.

"Babe, Landon is on the line. Ralph Goodwall died."

"Good. I hope he burns in the fire," she responded. Her voice was gargled and full of saliva. Without hesitation, Edward rose to his feet.

"Actually, I'm glad you're awake. Landon would like to talk to you. He wants to ask you something," Edward lifted his hand to his wife. His arm hung there, looking like a limb on a tree. She twisted her head like a dog and finally nabbed the phone away from him. She looked down at the screen, her strangled hair tilting with her head. Slowly she raised the phone to her ear and mouth.

"Yes?" she rasped.

"Sharon, dear, what do you mean fire?" Landon asked. Sharon's head began to bounce up and down, looking like a cat with a fur ball. She coughed continually until finally her head stopped bobbing.

"Scio colis lucem. Servies inimico scio. Quae nunc ego illam me pertinere," she growled. She took away the mobile from her head and walked into the kitchen. Edward stared in amazement at her rigid robotic like movement. She dropped the phone into the garbage disposal and flipped on the switch. A shattering sound escaped the sink. A tiny billow of smoke wisped out of the drain hole. Sharon turned off the disposal and began to walk in his direction.

He watched in bewilderment. Sharon walked, expressionless from the kitchen, through the living room, and into the hallway. Edward stood up. He followed behind her with his mouth agape. She had her arms stretched out from her sides, and her fingers slid against the walls. Her nails dug deep into the wallpaper, leaving long uneven scratch marks trailing behind her. She continued to walk slowly down the hallway, the pictures suddenly dispatched themselves from the walls. They left their hooks and shattered to the floor. The lights throughout the apartment began to flicker violently and wildly. Edward saw the bedroom door open on its own. It swung on its hinges as Sharon strolled inside. The door slammed loudly before Edward could reach it. Once again he banged on the door. Heavy pounds echoed off the wood. But there was no acceptance. She was ignoring him. He had no phone, and Sharon's was in the room with her. He leaned on the door screaming her name, until a force drove him back into the air, slamming him against the conjoining walls. Now, completely horrified, he ran out of his apartment into the narrow corridors of "Shangri-La Apartments." He slumped onto the floor, resting his back against the exterior of his home. He hoped Landon was on his way. Whatever words Sharon had growled at his friend, surely Landon would know this was no joke. A serious spiritual presence had manifested itself in his apartment. Edward knew in his heart that this wasn't a heavenly force either. This was no Travolta angel, or spirits from God to help the Los Angeles Angels win the World Series. This fear drove him to tears as he squatted against the wall in the hallway of his building. His mind reeled, trying to remember Bible verses or hymns. But all that his mind could produce was despair. A puddle of tears grew deeper on the floor as he wept.

8.

Sharon yanked open the drawer in the bathroom, housing her makeup. She found the darkest shade of lipstick and proceeded back into the bedroom. She felt driven. She knew something was controlling her; she had no will of her own. It was like being buckled into a rollercoaster, except this one seemed like it had no end. But an eternity of screaming, with drops and twists. The tracks would forever lay ahead of her, escalating her to her doom. She felt neither thirsty nor hungry, but revived. She had no desire except to accomplish what this presence was demanding. With both her hands stationed underneath the bedframe, she tipped the queen bed over, exposing the pearly carpet. She used the inky lipstick to draw an inverted star. She recognized it immediately as being a pentagram. Her hand gripped the lipstick firmly as her new driver finished the outer circle. Behind her own thoughts she heard a devilish voice. The voice was putrid and full of spit. *"This is for little Tony. You will finish the offering to Master, and serve us in the fire. The power fills you now, surges through you."*

Sharon gripped at the sides of her head, screaming. The voice was right, she did feel a power that she had never felt before. It was enticing and foreign. She knew that she must kidnap Tony, and fulfill this calling. Kill him and bathe in his blood upon the pentacle. When she thought of her husband, the voice bellowed again.

"I will kill him. Do you hear me wench? I will make sure the light does not rescue him."

"No!" Sharon screamed back. The presence elevated her off the floor and threw her against the closet doors, smashing them. Her body shook furiously as she lay on the floor. She felt sickly.

"Do you feel that? Feel my presence inside? I can give and take, as freely as I wish. Do not tempt me to end you."

Sharon Beard stood to her feet and swayed. This was too much strain on her body. She took a step towards the bedroom door. She tried to fight her driver, but she elevated again, flying into the television hanging on the wall beside her. She started to cough. Blood rained out from behind her lips. Little drops pelted the floor.

9.

What seemed like endless hours, but was in reality only about thirty-five minutes, Edward looked up and saw Landon. The black man was clothed in a dark clerical suit and somber top hat. Rain water dripped off the brim and dried onto his broad shoulders. As he made his approach, the beige walls and brown carpet clashed with his color scheme. The man resembled a reaper, or harbinger of death, floating across a desert sea. Edward stood to his feet and looked his friend in the eyes. A small glimmer shone within them.

"Hello Edward, are you okay?" he asked, giving his friend a hug.

"I'm fine, but Sharon, she"-

He held up his hand to mute the discussion. Edward fell silent.

"She spoke Latin to me," replied Landon, pulling a Bible out from behind his coat. Dangling around his neck, was a rosary. Edward stared at it.

"What did she do?" questioned Landon.

"She cut her palms, and with the blood, wrote a name all over the mirror."

"What was the name?"

"Agnes," replied Edward. Landon dropped his eyes to the fuzzy floor. He closed them as if in deep thought, or subtle prayer. "Agnes; it is a very historical witch name," he said, opening his eyes. "The self-mutilation to her palms, is to mock Christ's wounds."

Edward felt the hallway dip as if in a wave. He coughed slightly, trying to fight his despair. Landon put his hands on his friend's shoulders.

"If I am correct, there are things we must clarify before we go in," he said.

"What?" cried Edward. "She could be dying!" he pushed his friend's arms away. Landon held out his rosary. "I see you looking at this," he said.

"Yes."

"Do you believe Christ died for you?"

Edward stared blankly at his friend. Then asked, "What does that have to do with anything?"

"What's going on inside of your wife, is spiritual psychological warfare. If she is truly being oppressed, the demon must know and recognize Christ in you. Sharon must recognize love. What do scriptures say Christ is? Love."

"Okay," replied Edward. "I don't go to church anymore though. You know that."

"That has nothing to do with it. Your wife has to feel loved and wanted. She has to want to break free from the attaching spirit," said Landon. Edward took in a deep breath. This was all too much, but he knew in his heart that his friend was right. "Okay Landon."

Landon flipped through a couple pages of his Bible. He closed it shut. He looked his friend in the eyes once more. "No matter what happens in there, you stay strong. Do not give ground to fear. The spirit will sense this and try to invade you. Please do all that I say and follow my lead."

"I can do that," answered Edward.

"Most of all my friend, stay strong. I've only done one of these before. A few years back, I was on a mission's trip to Chile. A woman and young child had been possessed. I was able to free them both, but the boy died the next day. But this is different and I believe Sharon will be all right. So should you," said Landon. They both turned to the door. Edward opened it slowly as darkness crept out from the opening. Landon followed his friend into the apartment. The entire space was swollen in heavy darkness. The room was chilly. The two men moved slowly as if they were becoming frozen. Edward thought they would turn into human popsicles before he could save his wife. The lights flickered sporadically, exposing a mess that had transpired while Edward was outside.

"You heard none of this?" Landon asked, as he made his way deeper into the abode.

"No," replied Edward. He picked up one of the bar stools. The residence had been strewn as if by a chaotic tornado. Furniture was flipped and tables smashed. Every picture of the couple that was framed around the home, had been broken, and faces disfigured. The lights continued to strobe and Edward felt like he was in the ashes of a demonic apocalypse. It was strange to feel alien in your own home.

10.

The pair crossed into the living room. They breathed deeply and calmly. Surprisingly Edward wasn't scared, but freezing. He tried not to shake and to remain focused. Sharon appeared out from the dancing shadows. Her red fiery hair draped over her face. It was stringy and messy. Her veins on her arms and neck bulged. She looked sickly. The dress was fading and losing color. It looked as if it was deteriorating into her skin. Edward could almost see right through the fabric to her nipples. He broke the silence, "Honey, Landon is here. He…"

"He doesn't belong. He doesn't belong here," she growled, interrupting her husband. Landon took a step closer to her. He could sense and see that in fact something was oppressing her. She stood her ground as he approached. She cocked her head in a sideways tilt. The room still flashed as the lights continued their strobe.

"Sharon, can you hear me?" asked Landon, finally placing his hand inside his coat.

"No! She doesn't want to talk right now. Leave or I will kill her!" she rasped. Landon removed the Bible from his person. "I want to speak to Agnes."

"Ego sum. In tenebris est. Lux est hic repraesentet," Sharon bellowed in a hateful voice. Edward wanted to attack, but he knew he had to wait for Landon's order. He wanted his wife well again and for that to happen he had to let this unfold.

"Yes, I know there is much darkness here," said Landon. "Edward. Restrain her!"

He leaped onto his wife tackling her. She screamed in a throaty, bloody wail. Her shrieks were high pitched and full of saliva. Edward smelled a putrid odor, but he held her down. She kept screaming in Latin. "Die illa erit! Invocabo obscurum; get de! Get de!"

He pinned her arms behind her torso. He locked them in a brutal hold so she couldn't move. She had become strong, but he held tight.

"Leave my wife alone! Get the fuck out of my wife!" he demanded, as she struggled. She turned her head sideways and laughed, "I'm your wife now." He held on tighter as Landon flipped through pages of his Bible. The room was now completely icy and the shadows conjured up beside the trio. Edward placed his lips on her ear. “I love you Sharon, ever since that first dance. Remember the club,” he whispered. Landon started the exorcism.

“In the name of the Father, the Son and the Holy Spirit, I call upon you to leave this woman. In Christ’s name and upon my duty, we command you to depart from us. You unclean spirit”-

“No! Blasphemer; et non salvabo eam!” Sharon wailed. Landon towered over her. “You will release her!” He saw movement in her stomach beneath the fabric of the dress. As if something crawled under her skin. The fabric had almost seeped all the way though her skin and into her. Suddenly a face emerged on the lower part of her chest, beneath her breasts. It was ugly and looked to be screaming. It disappeared as quickly as it had come. Landon continued the ritual. He raised his arms to the ceiling.

“All satanic powers, leave this woman,” he commanded, removing the rosary from his throat. Sharon struggled against her husband and screamed in anguish. Edward still held her securely. “You depart from her! You hear me?” Edward demanded, “You hear me? Leave her alone!”

Her body shook uncontrollably. This was followed by horrible coughing. Landon snapped his Bible shut and snatched a flask of holy water from inside his coat. He splashed it around the three of them. Sharon began to pant, as the coughs turned into heaves. Landon threw the flask away and panned the room.

“Do you have a chest or box?” he asked. “She’s going to throw the unclean spirit up!”

Edward scanned the room frantically. His mind spinning as if on a tilt-a-whirl.

“There! Next to the couches, just throw our scrap books out!” he yelled.

Landon hurried to the chest. He spilled the contents quickly. The memories scattered out. Like bullets leaving the cartridge of a gun, all the memories hit Edward dramatically. Landon dropped the chest directly in front of Sharon. He gripped her by the hair and held her head over the opened chest. The heaving was rapid now, escalating into deep contortions. The dress had now been completely absorbed into her body. “Agnes, and all the unclean inhabitants of this body, I command you in the name of the Father to depart! Now!” commanded Landon.

The room became hollow and time seemed to slow to Edward. That same putrid horrible smell had invaded the entire apartment. Sharon was completely naked now, and on the verge of vomiting. Finally, in one last gut wrenching heave, she vomited the dress out of her body, into the chest. Landon dropped Sharon and jumped onto the chest, slamming the lid down.

“Is there a lock?” he screamed. But Edward was too busy crying over his motionless wife. Her eyes remained shut, and her skin still cold and pale. Landon stuck his rosary through the lid latch, locking the demonic dress inside.

11.

Edward held his wife in his sweaty arms. He panted and tears mixed with sweat stained his shirt. A strong dampness of dread had proceeded into his heart. Landon was still sitting on top of the chest, praying quietly. At last Sharon opened her eyes. Her pupils were brighter, radiating with hope.

“Sharon,” Edward said, “I’m so sorry. I’m sorry.” He gulped air fiercely. She squeezed his hand tightly. She tried speaking, but her voice was frail. Instead she mouthed, *“I love you.”* She looked over at Landon, who was now standing with the chest nestled between his right arm and body. She nodded her head towards him, *"Thank you."*

Landon dipped his head in approval. "Can you manage her okay to the bed?" he asked. Edward nodded and stood to his feet with Sharon in his arms. He carried her to the room and laid her gently on the bed. Her color was coming back to a light glow. Edward smiled. Somehow by Divinity, his wife had been saved. Landon stood in the doorway.

"It will take time for her body to heal," he said. Edward gave his friend a hug. The retired pastor left the Beard's apartment. The rain drizzled down on him as he drove home. The sun was coming up, turning the sky into a swirly shade of orange and purple. Life was beautiful.

Sometime later in the years that came, Landon passed away. As if fate was somehow controlled by omens of the dark, Landon died in his sleep, just like Mr. Goodwall. It would seem to Edward, as he sat in the church pews (every Sunday now) that good people usually punched out early. He had never spoken about the dress with Landon after what had happened. Same with Sharon; she could not recall any events of that night. Edward never asked either. Sometimes it was better to be ignorant in bliss, than miserable in knowledge.

It was a little into January of the following year, when Landon's son came from New York. He arrived to hold a yard sale at his father's house. Everything must go, no relic was to be left behind. His father and he had never really seen eye to eye. He was filled with grief on his father's passing, but it was more of grief over the cleanup. He was agitated with all the paperwork and hassle of traveling. He sold a rather odd looking chest to a girl who he planned on sleeping with that night. It was very old. He found it buried in the wall of his father's closet. She gave him the twenty dollar bill and her phone number. She drove away happy with her purchase and horny for what lay ahead that night. The afternoon sun shone down onto her smiling face. She drove away never recognizing what purchase she had just made. Her number would be up shortly.

Numbers

Of all the problems which will have to be faced in the future, in my opinion, the most difficult will be those concerning the treatment of the inferior races of mankind. – Leonard Darwin

1.

The murmur was loud, but came in different stages, as Tyler Shill sat in the waiting area. The room was filled with disgruntled, waiting people. Some chatted, others were on their phones, most laid their heads back and rested. It was an ordinary waiting room, all white, with some potted plants. Upon further investigation, Tyler learned the plants were fake. None of these people looked to be around the same age. Tyler thought it seemed rather full in the room. He guessed everyone must have gotten the same letter in the mail as he did. *Mr. Shill, please report to the number facility. Your presence is needed. If you disregard this post, it is in direct violation of California law.* Tyler chuckled to himself. California was a disastrous state. But he loved it just the same. He ran his hands through his brown peppery hair. Suddenly the man next to him spoke.

"Number forty-four was just called. I'm friggin ninety-six," he said, pointing to his chest. Tyler smiled at him. "Well, I'm one-hundred and eight! So you're closer than me."

The man smiled back at him. He had a couple years seniority on Tyler. He glanced at the receding hair line and beer belly. The man was dressed in overalls. Tyler's neighboring human in the chair turned his balding head away. A small hush began to invade the area as a man older than Tyler and number ninety-six, hurried up to the receptionist's counter. His body language properly read anger. He slammed his fists onto the counter.

"This is ridiculous! I have been waiting five hours! Why did I even receive this letter?"

A young girl sat behind the counter. She wore scrubs that were a deep white, almost milky. She had an hourglass figure. Her charcoal hair was tidied up in a bun. "Sir, go back to your seat," she insisted. "Please sir, we cannot answer any questions at this time."

The man shook his fists into the air, then pounded them onto the immaculate countertop. “That’s not good enough!” he hollered. The woman behind the counter stood to her feet. With a movement almost like a prance, she left the reception area. When she returned, a gentleman who looked to be in his early thirties, accompanied her. He had ebony slicked-black hair and emerald eyes. He wore a doctor’s coat that seemed odd. It was a dark shade, with white stitching. It was long and almost billowed like a cape as he walked.

“My name is, Dr. Vlad. What seems to be the problem, sir?” he asked, in a heavy accent. Tyler thought maybe Russian? Romanian? He decided to keep eavesdropping. Things could get interesting.

“Finally! Someone who can really tell me what the hell’s going on,” said the angry man. He turned his attention to the male doctor. “Why is my presence needed?”

“Well, you see, that is the state’s business and our company’s policy is not to discuss such matters if we’re not in private,” remarked the doctor. The angry man looked at him in a confused manner. One eyebrow lifted higher than the other one.

“Would you like all these other people, to know your business?” asked Dr. Vlad.

“No, I would rather not,” said the irate man. His body posture slumped a little. He was slowly losing his rage. “But I don’t have a lot of time! I want my questions answered now!”

The handsome doctor placed both hands on the man’s shoulders. He rubbed them firmly.

“Please, if you’d just follow me into one of the exam rooms. Then all of your questions will be answered,” replied the doctor.

“Truly?” asked the man.

"Yes, for you see, we have all the time in the world."

The young doctor nodded to the girl. She smiled in approval, or perhaps obedience, and sat back behind the counter. The doctor nudged the old, irritated man towards the saloon style doors, which led into a long corridor of exam rooms. "Do you have his file?" asked the doctor. The young girl handed him a clipboard paper clipped with documents. The two men left, disappearing behind the swinging doors.

As time unraveled, Tyler dozed off. Sure, he could have watched the big screen TV hanging on the wall, or get lost in the endless magazines littering every table top. But he didn't. No, instead he let the murmur of the room sway him off to sandy beaches, where naked ladies played in the sand and gave him back rubs. Where countless bottles of Jameson papered the shore. Then a fog horn started to blare. It bellowed out in a female's voice. She was yelling out a number. Instantly, Tyler awoke with a shake. He looked over at the gentleman who had been number ninety-six. He was long gone. Gone somewhere on the other side of the door. Now just an empty seat stared back at Tyler. Finally the girl who was refined and pleasing to the eye screamed his number. Tyler rose, stretched his arms out and yawned. He walked to the counter.

2.

When he made it to the counter, he placed his hands neatly on its surface. He gave the girl a big toothy grin. His cheeks were dented with dimples. With the smile still stuck on his face he said, "Hello, sweetie."

"Hello," she responded, ignoring eye contact. "Tyler Shill. Foreman, construction worker, handyman."

“Yes, that seems about right. Except for one thing,” he said.

She looked up from his file, finally making eye contact. “And what would that be, Mr. Shill?”

“Great lover,” he replied. A tiny smirk twisted upon her face. Then she looked away shaking her head. “Driver’s license please,” she said. He handed it to her. She studied the card and the computer in front of her. She pounded away on the key board like a stenographer.

“Everything checks out here. Date of birth ‘eighty-two,” she said, as she continued to bang away on the keys.

“Well yes, that is my birthday. Now can you tell me what I’m here for?” he asked.

“Didn’t you hear the doctor? They will provide you with all that information in the next room.”

“Look. I have a normal doctor that I see on the regular. He didn’t inform me”- he began, but she cut him off. “He should have! You see, that’s the problem nowadays. Nobody wants to see an idea through. No goal, or action is ever completed all the way through; never to one hundred percent!”

He stared at her a moment. Then smiled at her again. “Well, depends on what kind of action or goal you’re talking about. I mean I am pretty sure on the action I’d take with you.”

“Right,” her voice now tainted with scorn, “because I’m just going to open my legs right up for you. Now please, continue into room seven. The doctor will be with you shortly.”

Without any more witty remarks, Tyler left the waiting area into the long hallway. It was very glum and dingy. Nothing like the immaculate waiting area. Small bulbs dangled from the ceiling. They sputtered and buzzed annoyingly. After he walked for three minutes, a surge tore into the bulbs and the hallway glowed. Then, instantly the lights went back to a dreary, colored passageway. He opened up room seven and was greeted by an elevated, olive, exam table. Two stools were stationed around it, along with nitrous oxide and oxygen tanks. A small sink and cabinets were nestled in the corner. Long slender tubes hung from the ceiling. Tyler had never been in a patient room like this before. Something was chipping away at his mind about those tubes. A small voice was saying leave, but instead he sat on the exam table and waited.

3.

At last a female doctor came into the room. She had very pale, glass-like skin, inky hair tied into a bun just like the receptionist. In fact, this woman resembled the girl with the hour glass figure, in almost every way. All but the skin. Her epidermis was so white, that Tyler could only think of snow. As soon as she entered, an aroma alien to Tyler floated in with her. Her eyes were the exact color as the girl who had called his number. Both pupils twinkled, as if she had magic brewing behind them. Tyler was becoming aroused. Her legs were elegant stilts, and her voice was like a symphonic wave of harmony.

“Hello, Tyler,” she said. “My name is Dr. Tina Dark. Please remove your shirt; this will only take a few minutes.” She began to strike on the clipboard in her hands. Her hand swift as she used a pen to fill out his documents. He took off his shirt and could feel his face begin to flush. Inside his pants, an erection started to form. He had no idea why this woman was making him so aroused.

"Please, lie down Tyler," she motioned to the exam table. He lay on his back, hoping she would not notice his ever growing lump. He swallowed deeply.

"It's okay," she said, "it happens quite frequently. Here, please sign this." Tina Dark handed him the clipboard she had been scratching on. She went to the sink area and pulled a bottle out from the cabinet.

"What is this?" he asked. When she returned to him, she had a cotton ball dipped in some type of liquid. She looked down and saw that he had, in fact, already signed. "You are here because your regular doctor has selected you for our program. I am very sorry he did not inform you." She swabbed his forearms, almost instantly he felt them go numb. He smiled at her. "Well, if the program means taking more of my clothes off for you, then I'm game."

She ignored him at first and inserted a needle twice into both his forearms. Tina then guided the tubes from the ceiling, into his arms where the needles had been. Tyler felt a slight wave of panic wash into his brain. "What is this?" he screamed. She put a hand on his chest. She petted the hair that grew there. Now this time she smiled. "Some people think that flesh is sacred. Do you feel me petting you? Of course you do Tyler. How strong your tissue and muscle is. But blood is the alpha over the skin, no?"

She ran her hand down his stomach and into his pubic hair. He could feel her taunt his skin there, until finally grabbing his penis. He felt her clench around his erection. He let out a hysterical laugh and yelled, "Lady, what the fuck's the matter with you?" he tried to get up but she held him back.

"Time for the gas," she said, as she placed the mask over his nose and mouth. "Blood is honey. Your honey is flowing faster as I stroke you. Honey feeds many." She stroked him harder. Her hand fondling his erection. Then just on the verge of climax, she quit. Tyler was holding his breath, unbeknownst to her. "Don't fidget now," she said, "you'll damage my equipment. I'll be right back." She got up and walked towards the sink.

He felt his blood begin to be sucked out of his body. Somehow the tubes were draining him. The process was speeding up every second, with his forearms going completely asleep. He thrusted himself upward, and bent his face to his hands. Tyler ripped off the mask and let out a quiet breath. Tina was washing her hands in the sink. He realized he could still raise his arms. He lifted them up to his mouth. Using his teeth, he yanked out the wires in painful speed. Blood flowed from his forearms like a crimson waterfall. He shook them, trying to get them awake. Tyler knew he had little time. He proceeded across the polished surface of the exam room floor, and reached the doctor. He slammed Tina's head into the cabinets. A sharp crunch sounded, as her nose collided with the wood. She fell to the floor. Stumbling she tried to stand. Tyler kicked her in the stomach. She cried in pain and fell back on the floor. He kicked her one more time for good measure and escaped out of the exam room. He fell to the clammy floor of the dim hallway. Looking up he noticed tubes he hadn't before. They stuck to the ceiling, five in a row. A substance rushed through them. It resembled a dark, oily-red liquid. With this new discovery he managed himself to his feet. He started a staggered retreat, looking like a drunk on the best night of his life. But this was not going to be the best night. Tyler knew something horrible was hiding in the coming nightfall. He fled exhaustedly, looking for an exit, leaving nothing but scarlet lines behind him.

Dr. Tina Dark opened her eyes. She pulled out a headset from the pocket of her doctor's coat. She placed the mouth piece in front of her lips and straightened the head set on top of her ears and hair.

“Code Nine!” she screamed into the microphone stemming out in front of her mouth. She gasped in pain as she tried to stand. That sonofabitch Tyler, will pay for this. That maggot is going to get his. She promised herself that he would not live to see day. “Code Nine!” she yelled again into her headpiece.

“What floor?” a voice responded.

“Ground.”

“Patient did not go out through waiting. So the only way now, is up.”

“Exactly,” she said, “there is will he will die!”

Tina tried to stand again, but her injury flared. She screamed in anguish and remained on the floor. The kicks to her stomach were agonizing. Vlad was not going to be happy about this. Suddenly an orange light oscillated from the ceiling. A loud horn blared out into the facility. Tina smiled. That bastard would be caught, one way or another.

4.

Tyler fell again to his knees. The floor was icy and smooth. He laid there a moment trying to figure out what direction to take. Above his head, the bulbs turned a fiery orange and an alarm started to clang. He rose frantically and opened the nearest door. He tumbled in, his body floppily dancing into the room. He could feel himself growing weary. He scanned the room for a hiding place or exit. But all his eyes beheld was an image that in itself was appalling. He was standing in some kind of surgery room. But it was more of a human body chamber. He brought his hand to his mouth trying to hold back vomit. Hanging by large fish like hooks from the ceiling, were four men. One was the man number ninety-six. Next to his dangling corpse was the disgruntled man who had slammed his fists onto the counter. But now both his fists were missing, even his legs! His slowly decaying body showed signs of stitching where internal organs had been removed. As Tyler's eyes adjusted, he saw that the limbs of his waiting room neighbor were absent too. He swallowed back his urge to dispel his last meal and continued to search the room.

Along the sides of the ghastly place were surgical tools and hand saws. Countless knives and huge clear containers congregated atop tables. Behind the tables, positioned on the walls were large mirrors. A long sink and what resembled a trough sat at the end. A door was stationed there. Suddenly it opened. A person in a lab coat drenched in gore, rushed in, headed towards Tyler. The assailant wore goggles and a surgical mask. They carried a curved meat cleaver. Tyler couldn't tell their gender. He reached for the nearest knife (a butcher's knife) and ran towards the intruder. Using the knives almost like swords, they fought. Clangs and pings echoed with each knife striking the other. The attacker slit a gash into Tyler's shoulder, but Tyler knocked the cleaver away, finally holding the person at knife point. He let his enemy feel the cold blade on their neck. The person head-butted Tyler. He let go for a split second, but recovered just as fast. He grabbed the person again, and stabbed them in the neck. He thrust the butcher knife from one side of the neck, to the other.

Tyler looked up and saw himself in one of the mirrors. His arms held nothing. He looked back down at the person bleeding in his arms. He cocked his head back up in a jolt. The person in his arms had no reflection, but was completely invisible in the mirror. He dropped the body from his grasp. He located some surgical tape and using the knife, he cut his pants into shorts. He fastened a tourniquet on both his arms, using his belt, pant remains, and the string. He fled the room of horrors, but as he exited, he thought he heard the deceased attacker talk. Couldn't be; it was just his mind playing tricks on him. His blood was growing thinner. This was no time to hallucinate. He was back in the wailing corridor. The alarm cry sounded just like a newborn child. He came to some stairs and started to climb them. He hoped that what lay ahead would be his sanctuary.

5.

The fear burned intensely inside Tyler as he climbed the stairwell. His body was becoming drained, and the pain bloomed like a magnificent flower. The alarm was piercing his eardrums with every step he took. He went up five flights, finally reaching the top. At the end of the dreary corridor was one room. The door was silver and no light shone from underneath. He hustled down the ever-stretching hallway; he pleaded in his mind that surely this was a way out. He reached the door and grabbed the horizontal handle. He pulled out towards him and entered the new room. A bright light blinded him at first and then he screamed in terror.

Inside, the young doctor Vlad, was seated on a throne. It was a noir color, and was decorated in skulls. A red puffy cushion was centered in the middle. Vlad wore a cape atop his shirtless body, with velvet pants. Two identical women stood on each side of him. Each woman looked exactly like Tina Dark and the cute receptionist. But these two were naked, and they were rubbing Vlad's shoulders and legs. Cast out before him and his throne were many women, who just like all the other girls Tyler had seen, were identical. They were all nude and frolicking with each other. Some were having sex with one another; some participated solo. But Tyler vomited when he saw what was shooting out from the ground. Little sprinklers blanketed the space the women sat or laid on. Blood arched out from the sprinkler heads, drenching the herd of gorgeous naked women. The girls stretched out underneath the waves. Some drank directly from the spigot. They sucked on the head as the blood shot into their mouths. Others bathed in it, and licked the flowing waves off their partner, or partners.

When they noticed Tyler, they scowled and hissed at him. They bared their teeth. Their mouths opened in big toothy snarls. They had *fangs!* Suddenly, Tyler was pushed from behind. He fell face first onto the slippery blood pooled floor. The door slammed shut behind him, locking him inside. Vlad rose from his throne. All the women stood as well. Their sole attention on the intruder, who entered into their place of feeding. Vlad began to laugh. It was a dark evil chuckle, which grew in volume. The laugh bellowed into Tyler's ears in deafening decibels. That was the last thing Tyler Shill ever heard.

6.

Two weeks later, the young doctor Vlad stood over Tyler's grave. The night was cold. A bitter wind swept into the graveyard. Heavy pregnant rain clouds blocked the full moon. The slithery creatures of the night, climbed out of the crevices and across the grass. An older black man stood accompanying the doctor.

"Good evening, Vlad," he said. A chill blew over them.

"Hello Harold. This one almost discovered us. If he had gone down one different hallway, he may have, in fact, escaped our grasp."

"But he didn't," replied Harold. "We have done this for thousands of years. It has happened, but we always contain it. Always."

Vlad looked up at the sky. It was calling him; he always felt free when he was up there.

"They're getting smarter," said Vlad. "And populating quicker."

Harold ran his huge hands through his brown mane resting on his head. He then pulled on his beard as if holding back something. "Did my men do their job correctly? I know last month we had some trouble."

"Yes," said Vlad. "There isn't a body buried beneath us. Empty coffin as always. And as always the body parts are shipped upstate to your brotherhood."

"Good," replied Harold. "The council will be pleased. The new laws have greatly established our domain. The humans are multiplying rapidly, but with our brothers at the helm of each state; I believe we can rest and feed easy."

The clouds dispersed and Harold groaned. He twitched as hair sprouted out all over his body. His nose started to expand into a snout. Large pulsing veins bulged on his skin. He was transforming. Vlad smiled.

"I always like to watch," he said, as Harold turned into a werewolf. The beast scampered off into the trees beyond the cemetery. Vlad jumped into the air and felt his body downsize and arms morph into wings. He successfully integrated into his other form. The clouds greeted him as his bat-body soared. He flew over a deep tranquil pond. Vlad swooped down, gliding close to the water's surface. He was hungry. He left the isolation of the countryside and headed back to the city. Some of that red sauce sounded delightful.

The Pond

Humans are amphibians - half spirit and half animal. As spirits they belong to the eternal world, but as animals they inhabit time.

– C.S Lewis

1.

The wind swept through the spruce trees fiercely. Its icy touch sent shivers down Eden's spine. She held onto her warm coffee with shaking hands. She told herself that fifty-five degrees wasn't cold for a summer night in Colorado. It was nine o'clock and the night was young. Her flight had landed twenty minutes ago, and she was happy to be back on the ground. Her father, Bill, wasn't usually late. She waited outside to get away from the annoying bustle inside the airport's stomach. In fact, all of the people moving around in there did remind Eden of stomach indigestion. She sipped her coffee with vanilla cream and perched on a wooden bench. She reminisced about her father. Her childhood had been decent until the divorce. But what had once bothered her, now was just a relic of what seemed an ancient time. Past dwelling was not good for the brain or heart. Progression was never behind, always present and forward. The coffee slithered down her throat, giving her a little relief from the obnoxious wind. Setting her coffee down, she rubbed her arms. Her red sweater was doing no justice. She decided to go back inside, when she saw her dad's truck rumbling into the parking lot. The old Bronco sputtered and groaned as it traveled across the pavement. She waved. Her dad saw her and returned the gesture with a smile.

Bill pulled up next to the curb. His smile was bright and kind. He had not seen his daughter in five years. He reminded Eden of an old, happy Santa in the red Bronco. His snowy beard and bald head began to flush as she climbed in. She was excited, but also nervous. Her father had been diagnosed with lung cancer. Bill was an avid chain smoker. He sucked on those tobacco sticks as if they were Jolly Ranchers. Eden remembered the smell and the rotting odor in the house as a child. Finally when she was thirteen her mother divorced him. Now she sat next to him and gave Bill a sideways hug.

"Hello, sweetie," he croaked. He threw the truck into drive and the pair started to descend the hill away from the airport. "How have you been, kiddo?"

"Good," she answered, "just graduated you know."

"College is next. Are you excited?" he asked. He watched the beam of the headlights cutting through the night. He scanned the sides of the road, remembering that animals were always jumping out.

"Yes, but kind of nervous. I did want to take a break off from school in general. Maybe for a year. But Mom won't let me."

Bill sighed. He coughed a little. They turned up Main Street. He pulled over to the side and parked parallel in front of a drug store. Eden looked up at the sign. Homer's Drug was a very popular drugstore with its burger joint in the back. Or that's what the lady at the airport had suggested. But she knew this was a stop for cigarettes.

"Do you want anything for the cabin? I got some stuff, but I'm not sure what you wanted," he asked, getting out of the truck. He kept smiling at her.

"No thanks Dad, I'll be okay. You know you should quit. Kind of why I'm here, remember?"

"Ah, sweetie, I thought you were just here to visit your old pops. I called you because I wanted you here," he said, as he slammed the heavy metal door. She groaned and watched her father cross the street and into the door of Homer's. She did wonder why he had called her. They rarely spoke and now, perhaps because of the cancer, he was trying to rekindle lost years. Eden peered out the window as a man with a Doberman dog traveled past. She wondered if her dad had any pets.

Bill Maxon hurried inside. He nodded to Gary at the counter. He was thirty years younger than Bill, but he had grown fond of the boy. Bill didn't have a son, and Gary was a funny twenty-four year old squirt. He always wanted to meet Eden, but Bill purposely left her in the car. There was no need for them to meet. Not at the moment. More pressing matters needed attending. He bustled throughout the tiny store, headed towards the fishing area. He scanned the rows of poles and walls of promising bait. Each container said "Fish Guarantee." Bill thought what a bunch of mumbo jumbo. For the past year, living on Chorus Pond, he had always caught trout three ways. One was worms; those little wriggly creatures always drew the fish in. Two, were hook flies, and three, salmon eggs. He smiled as he stood observing the tools for fishing. It had been a great pastime. Gary appeared next to him, startling the old man.

"Hi, Bill!" he exclaimed. "Fishing at ol' Chorus Pond, eh?"

Bill turned to look at the young man. Gary had straight long hair that gripped the sides of his head like twine on a bale of hay. It went so far as to stick all the way to his neck. Gary pushed the bangs out of his face and smiled. Bill thought he looked like an idiot in his Homer's Drug apron.

"Yeah, man. You know it's been nice living up there," Bill replied.

"I don't know how you can sleep up there, Bill. With all the frog voices," said Gary, stepping behind the counter that Bill had his elbows resting on.

"It's not that bad. Peaceful. It was my father's, you know. Had to get out of Durango after the divorce. Wound up here."

"It's a nice cabin. But Bill, is it haunted?" asked Gary, intrigued.

"Don't be such a nut. Ghosts aren't real."

"But I've heard stories, especially about a fro..."Gary tried, but Bill cut him off by raising his hand. "There's worse things than a stupid campfire tale of a spirit living in the pond. Now I'll take some salmon eggs, and a cup of worms." Gary nodded in approval. He grabbed the jar of salmon eggs from beneath the glass counter. He turned to the small, black-box fridge behind him. Checking the dates on the white foam containers, he found the right one for Bill and hurried up front to meet his customer and friend.

2.

Bill watched the clerk scurry to the counter. He liked watching him work hard. This kid wasn't like today's youth: stuck to screens and always trying to get something for nothing. Gary understood hard work and determination. He wasn't lazy and knew a thing or two, about fishing and cars. He had helped Bill with the Bronco a few times. Bill knew the man might make a good suitor for his daughter. But Bill had other plans festering in the back of his mind. Gary began to punch away on the register.

"Gary, if you had a chance at immortality, to keep living, would you take it?" asked Bill.

"That's a strange question. What's the price?" inquired Gary, bagging the items. "There's always a price."

"Love."

"Well, what's the point in living forever, if you never have love again?"

"Well, what I meant I guess, is sacri..."Bill started, but the door of the store swung open. An angry Eden stood at the mouth of Homer's. Gary's eyes flashed with excitement. The moment he had been waiting for. "Dad! Please don't buy anymore cigarettes!" she commanded, walking in. Her sneakers released a squish sound against the tile as she walked. "Gary, this is my daughter, Eden."

Gary sprang from around the counter. He scanned for other customers. Noticing they were the only ones in the store he held out his hand. It shook slightly. He peered into her aqua eyes. Her mouth spread into a smile. Her hair was blonde and bright, like the sun. His mouth quivered until he finally calmed his nerves. "Hello Eden. Nice to meet you. Your dad has said wonderful things about you."

"Nice to meet you, Gary. Oh, so this old man actually talks about me?"

Bill told her, "Yes, dear, now look, no cigarettes. Go get back in the truck. I'll be out right now."

She started to leave, when Gary called out, "Would you like to come back for a burger with me sometime?"

She turned and winked at him, "Maybe," she said. "If this old man here, removes my chastity belt."

Bill's face turned as red as a ripe tomato. He returned his attention back to Gary; who stood behind the counter, adding up the total price of the purchase.

"What's the damage?" Bill asked.

"Fourteen, ninety-six."

"Throw in a pack of Camels," growled Bill, shaking his shiny bald head.

3.

Eden sat with her arms angrily crossed over her chest. As the pair rolled through town, she made sure not to look in her father's direction. Bill scowled. Why were children so difficult? He turned off Pine Avenue and headed down a dirt road. Chorus Pond was located up Frog Mountain and nestled behind its peak. Bill's father had acquired the cabin there, and after many years of professional truck driving and a divorce, Bill found it to be humble and a place of tranquility. The solitude and whispers of nature were quite satisfying. As they moved higher up the mountain, large aspens waved their leaves as the Colorado breeze swept through the branches. He looked over at his daughter. "There's no need to be angry."

Eden shot him a sour look, the same one his wife used to make. She threw her hands up in the air. Her face turning into a bitter snarl. "Sure there is! You're killing yourself! Is that why you called me to come visit? Just so I can watch you die?" Eden crossed her arms back over her chest. She peered coldly out the window, pouting. Her dad chuckled a raspy laugh. He choked a little and then cleared his throat. "You're just like your mother. No, honey, I called you because I wanted to spend some time with you before college. Pretty soon you will be all moved away and on your own. I wanted to see you before that. You used to love to fish as a little girl, and now look, I live on a pond!"

The forest started to engulf the truck. It grew denser and greener. The towering trees moaned in the wind. Some of their limbs scratched the sides of the truck. Eden turned, giving her father her full attention. Tears welled up inside her eyes, "You bought cigarettes."

Bill shook his head, as if recovering from a nasty memory. "Honey, I've found a way to prolong my life despite the cancer. I'm going to be alright. I'm not climbing my stairway to heaven yet." He smiled at her, waiting to see if she got the joke. She did. “I don’t want to play that game,” she replied. Still smiling Bill said, “You used to love our Led Zeppelin game. What happened? Too much Miley in your life now?” he chuckled again and choked on spit.

“Fine, I guess I’ll just have to ramble on,” she said.

“Until the levee breaks,” he said.

“And I fly over the misty mountains,” Eden said gleefully.

“Where you become dazed and confused.”

“Until I wind up in the ocean with four sticks,” she replied.

Bill pursed his lips and spat out the window. “You cheated.”

“I said I didn’t want to play, Dad.”

“Doesn’t matter, we’re here,” he replied as he parked the Ford.

4.

Bill hopped out of the Bronco with a jig. He hustled across his lush front lawn and ascended to the patio. Eden never saw him move so fast in her life. She wiped the tears from her eyes and exited the Ford. The log cabin sat in a clearing between two huge spruce trees. It was a small, two bedroom cabin. The size was perfect for its peacefulness and its beautiful surroundings. Her nose tickled at the scents of the wilderness. The scenery was majestic beneath the moon. It was almost like an elegant painting, suitable for a postcard. Chorus Pond lay directly behind the cabin. Its murky depths mirrored the moonlight, giving a dark lunar gloom to its surface. Then she heard the frogs. Their croaks and chirps engulfed the night. Their sounds were joyous and prideful. Their voices suffocated the area in an orchestra of delight. This was nature untouched.

She tugged on her suitcase and started up the steps. With each step, the suitcase banged loudly as it climbed. She studied the porch before going inside. A wicker rocker sat in the corner. A metal bucket of empty Coors cans kept it company. The railings stationed around the deck had vines escalating their exterior. The floor had a few rugs and a mat by the front door. Then she noticed something else. She left her suitcase and proceeded across to the other side of the porch.

Before her, stretched out and heading to the end of the porch, were footprints. They seemed funny. She knelt, discovering a mucus and wetness that covered them. There were five toes. The shape of the appendages was slender. Inside the mold of the print, were what looked like indents of bumps, and what may have been webbing between the toes. The size of the prints indicated that it must be bipedal. She placed her foot next to the print. It was only slightly larger than her own. What kind of animal could do this? Or perhaps it was her own father's? No, impossible, not with its weird shaped long toes. The prints continued over to the railings and then disappeared. Eden followed them to the very end and found a handprint on the banister. This print was different from the feet. It had four appendages. The gooey substance bathed it.

Suddenly, she felt a hand on her shivering shoulder. She gasped and turned around to be met with her father's brown eyes. They held confusion and tenderness. She buried her head into his chest. His smoke smell encased her.

"You scared the shit out of me!" she declared, her voice muffled against his chest. He held her away from him. He chuckled a raspy laugh. The porch seemed to grow into a dark shade as a cloud passed over the moon.

"I'm sorry, honey. What were you looking at?" he asked.

"What kind of animal could make these? Last time I checked, your toes were normal."

"Ah, those prints have been popping up recently. I'm not sure, I um, I really don't think it's a big deal. I'm not too worried about them. It's just nature." He smiled at her. Still perplexed, she walked back across the porch; following her father, they strolled inside. Eden's nose crinkled. The scent of the home was saturated with incense and burnt ash. She quickly retired to her room to bathe. The shower was warm, Eden cranked the handle all the way to the left, but it remained only warm. She decided it felt better than the coldness that plagued her outside, but she missed the scalding water of her own shower. Bill had running water and power, but it wasn't great here. There was no cable, no internet. He told her that the concerns of the world were not his. And only occasionally did he read the paper, or watch the news. He described that on Monday and Friday nights, he would meet Gary for dinner and beers. There is where he would watch any TV.

Gary seemed like a funny boy. He had made Eden laugh, and his voice was sexy. Just that hair of his needed a tame. He reminded Eden of a dorky boy she knew in school. Not really her type, but perhaps she would see Gary again for that burger. An elk burger did sound delicious. She stepped out of the shower. The overhead fan hummed loudly like a purring cat. She wrapped a blue striped towel around her body and began to comb at her wet, knotted hair. After a few moments, she switched the fan off and continued to comb. From outside the confines of the bathroom, she heard Bill talking. It sounded as if her dad was talking to company.

"No," he was saying, "not tonight. I said not tonight. I told you, this takes time." She didn't hear any response. Silence swept down the hallway. Who could he be talking to? Then she heard her father again. "It's fine. A promise is a promise."

Eden ditched her towel for her robe, and hustled into the hallway heading to the living room. She found her dad by himself. Nobody else stood in the room besides Bill and herself. He looked puzzled, Bill titled his head. "Yes, dear?" he asked.

"Who were you talking to?"

"Myself; you know, talking to myself about quitting."

"But I thought you said that didn't matter anymore? You found a solution," she said.

"Eden, you've had a long flight; get some rest. I'll have an excellent breakfast for you in the morning."

Still confused and somewhat disgruntled, she said goodnight and walked back to the bathroom. Something loomed dark in her brain. An urgency. Something of a warning started to scream for attention. But she ignored this feeling and laid in bed comfortably. The lullaby of frogs floated her to sleep peacefully.

5.

When Eden awoke in the morning, the smell of bacon and syrup flared in her nostrils. The aroma was sweet and mouthwatering. Her father still had his cooking skills. She sat up in the bed and rubbed her eyes. The voices of the frogs had become silent. Now only the winged birds of the Colorado countryside cried out. She got to her feet and discarded her robe. Squatting in front of her suitcase, she pulled out a pair of red and white panties, a pair of jeans, and a Nirvana band shirt. She used the bathroom, checked the latest social media on her phone, using up her data, which caused her cellphone to die. She plugged it into the outlet by the bed and headed down the hallway. Her spirit was rested. The sense of warning had subsided. No longer did she feel the need to flee. There was no longer a feeling of despair. Her father smiled at her as she entered the kitchen. He had on a black checkered flannel and denim pants. Sunlight poured in from the window above the sink, bathing him in a golden glow. His record player sitting on the living room window sill, played Gary Jules. She recognized the song "Mad World". Her mouth watered as she watched him add honey and banana pieces to the batter of the waffles. On the kitchen bar sat bacon, over easy eggs, and ingredients to make flavored tea. The kitchen had booth seating, protruding out from the wall in the right corner. The whole kitchen resembled an old-sixty's diner, except with a lumberjack feel. Eden slid into the booth.

"Everything smells amazing," she said, scanning the table before her. Her father walked over carrying three platters of food. He sat them down in front of her and bustled over to the other counter. He did not reply to her observation.

"How'd you sleep, Dad?" she asked. He poured a steamy cup of tea, fresh from the stovetop, and placed it in front of his daughter. He sat down. He was acting nervous.

"Not too shabby," he finally replied. His lips quavering for a cigarette. "Now, eat up and drink up. Good tea, excellent tea."

Eden poured syrup over her bacon and waffles. The scent was so intoxicating that she cut into it hastily. She gobbled it down, as if she was stranded and had found food for the first time. Bill watched her closely; he barely nibbled at his breakfast. He didn't touch his tea. Stopping for a moment, Eden asked, "What is it?" But Bill shook his head and returned to his food. She took the warm cup in her hands and smelled the tea. It was a lemon scent with a twist of something sweet. She couldn't ascertain what the smell was, as if something was disguising it. She brought the cup to her lips and felt the liquid wash down her throat and into her stomach. It was delicious. It sent a warm fuzzy feel throughout her body. She took another sip and forked at her eggs. She could feel the weight of the food on her fork, but something didn't seem right. The eggs started to slide a certain way, and they looked hazy. She felt her eyelids flutter and her head began to spin. Her body started to sway. With her failing eyesight the last thing she saw was her dad standing to his feet. She slipped off the booth and onto the kitchen floor. It was a mad world indeed.

6.

When she regained sight, she was looking up into her father's hairy chin. She realized she was on her back and that he was carrying her. They were outside; the scent of dew and pine cones washed over her. She tried to speak, but was still groggy. Finally Bill stopped walking. She found her voice. "Dad," she whispered, "what is going on?" But Bill ignored her and stood gazing forward. He bent down and placed his daughter softly on the ground. Her bare feet sank into the cold, sticky mud. They were on the edge of Chorus Pond. She rested on her side, trying to prop herself up on one elbow. Her mind and eyesight continued to go in and out of focus. She could only whimper soft words up to her standing father. But Bill ignored her, and did not stand her back up. She let her head roll to the side, and as it drooped, she tried to scream. But only a muffled cry escaped her mouth. Standing directly across from them was an animal, or perhaps a man. Her sight became a little less dense and with this new clarity she saw a creature standing like a man. It was a little shorter than her father and stood hunched, breathing deeply. Every time it drew a breath, a large sack hanging around its neck inflated. Its eyes were yellow and oval. They extended on the top and side of the creature's head. Its lime-white skin shined in the sunlight. Eden saw black spots on its legs. She continued to stare in amazement and wonder. The fingers and feet featured amphibian textures. It wore nothing and carried nothing.

"This is the offering?" it bellowed, in a deep resonating tambre.

She thought the creature sounded male. Bill nodded slowly. "Yes, I told you I promised. Do you have what you claim?"

"Yes, Bill, I have your salvation."

"Who are you?" asked Eden, in a small voice.

"I am the Keeper of the Pond," it answered. "Some of your kind call me The Frogman."

Eden wanted to laugh, to cry hysterically, but whatever drug was in her body would not let her. Nor would it let her retreat. Her mother was never going to believe this. Her eyesight began to lose focus again. But even as this sense was fading, her other four were working in overdrive. She heard The Frogman begin to cough. His pouch enlarged in size and from his throat a heavy, disgusting, hacking sound erupted. Her sight came back and she saw him vomit up a white, spherical object. It plopped onto the lake's shore.

"Here is the cure," The Frogman said. Bill stepped over his paralyzed daughter and picked it up. The object was covered in The Frogman's bile, but was extremely light.

"Pretend it's a big ball of food, Bill. Cut into it, eat it," instructed The Frogman.

The round object resembled a baseball, but the coloring was pure. It even left a snowy residue on Bill's fingertips as he held it. A smile stretched from ear to ear across his face.

"Thank you," Bill said. He turned away from The Frogman and knelt next to his daughter. A few tears dripped from his eyes.

"I'm sorry honey," he said, "but he claims I'll get you back. He just needs your help with something. A favor is a favor, princess." Bill kissed her on the cheek. He hiked his way back from Chorus Pond with his new prized possession in hand. Still groggy, Eden tried to crawl away, or stand, but she couldn't. Then to her horror, The Frogman's arms scooped her up from the muddy, Colorado earth. A slime climbed onto her as he carried her. His aroma was fishy and foul. Eden fainted and was lost to the mercy of the Keeper of the Pond.

A little stab of guilt gutted Bill as he entered his home. This brief self-loathing was washed away by what he grasped in his hands. He had met The Frogman five months ago and together they had come to a mutual agreement. The Frogman promised that Bill's daughter would be returned to him and that he held the cure for his cancer. Bill did not want to die; he knew that Eden still had many more years to live, and he wanted that too.

He went into the kitchen and placed the white orb onto a plate. He snatched a fork out from the drawer. He stood perplexed as he faced The Frogman's present. He stared until he finally realized that this was reality and that this was what he wanted. He couldn't go back now. He had just dealt with a mystical creature and joined in a child offering. He shook his head as if this movement would banish the scene from his memory. Carefully and tenderly, he cut into the ball. The fork slid through its outer skin and into the substance smoothly. A chunk left its form and flipped over onto the plate. He stabbed it and raised the morsel to his face; studying it.

The smell was sweet and tangy, almost fruity. He counted to five and stuck the morsel into his mouth.

Bill chewed, paused, and then chewed again. The piece seeped with a mango taste that made his tongue dance with flavor. He swallowed. It was pleasant. The Frogman hadn't instructed him on how much to ingest, so he took another bite. The same orgasmic mango taste swirled around his mouth. Suddenly, the orb disintegrated, and a sour pain punched his stomach. Bill stumbled to the floor crying and contorting in pain. It felt as if his intestines had exploded. Death was here for him; he had been tricked by The Frogman. He now realized his mistake: this was not salvation from a disease, but an expressway straight to Hell. Bill laid face first on the icy tile. He would forever, never, smoke again.

7.

Three months had passed since the discovery of Bill Maxon's death. Eden Maxon was nowhere to be found. Authorities and Detective Mumford, had given up the search. Gary would not stand for this. He set his kickstand on his dirt bike and stood in front of Bill's house. The home had been seized by the bank until further negotiations with his ex-wife resumed. But she was quite hysterical at the moment, due to her daughter's disappearance. Gary stood watching the house, as if by magic, Eden would come walking out. He wished he could have told his friend, Bill, goodbye, or possibly stopped him from dying. The official report said that his stomach had ruptured due to a substance that was ingested. Two parts of the intestines exploded. They called it suicide. Gary did not believe this. Bill was a strong, courageous man, someone that Gary looked up to, even if sometimes the man made mistakes. Bill had shown him a picture of Eden a few months ago. It was that picture that ignited a fiery desire in Gary's heart. He believed that Bill was not capable of such an act, the act of suicide.

He had heard the two legends surrounding Chorus Pond. The first was a story about a young man who drowned in the pond while drunk. His ghost was said to now haunt the pond and all its visitors. The other tale was of a creature, neither beast nor man, primitive, but not entirely. The legend went that a creature resembling an amphibian-humanoid, stalked the area and was known as the Keeper of the Pond. Gary had an inclination to find this story truthful, over ghosts. Especially since Bill had been talking about immortality the night Eden arrived. If Bill had somehow gotten mixed up with this creature or if Eden was simply lost at the pond, Gary was going to find her. He had to. He tugged on the backpack that hung from his shoulders and started his way towards the house. With him he carried trail mix, a compass, a flashlight, a bottle of water, and 9mm gun.

He ducked under the police tape. He walked up the steps and entered the home. The smell was stale and stinky. He saw the fridge had been left open. He examined the kitchen. Fresh footprints were on the floor and the fridge handles were covered in a slime. This residue was fresh too. Gary felt a surge of excitement. The legend was true! He knew he was taking a big leap of faith, but there was no way the detectives had missed this. These new discoveries had to have been only be from this morning. The prints led out the back door. Once he reached the edge of the forest, the tracks disappeared. He spied a Coke can about five feet away from him, and beyond that a chip bag. So the perp had been hasty and not taken the time to cover his trail. Gary broke into a jog, headed for the west bank of the pond.

Nearing the pond, he stopped jogging. He slowly came to a walk. He hadn't seen a clue or any food remains for twenty minutes. His walk finally came to a halt, as he crouched to catch his breath. He realized something he hadn't before. There were no sounds at Chorus Pond. The body of water was as silent as a tomb. No frogs sang, no birds chirped, not even the water's surface stirred. He opened his water bottle and took a swig. He gazed out of the forest and stared at Chorus Pond. He noticed some brush and trees had fallen down. He tossed the bottle back into his backpack and hustled over to the shore.

Branches and bushes were torn apart and dug up. The foliage had been built, almost molded, into a kind of housing or shelter. The same slimy residue was present, but applied heavier, and had the consistency of mud. He looked over on the other side of the clump and saw a plate with an apple and banana. A Coke can was nestled in the dirt. Gary began to rip apart the branches and bushes. The sun was high in the sky and its rays shined down onto a buried Eden Maxon. She lay encased in a jelly sack. The substance was clear, but sticky. Gary stared in horror, but saw that she was breathing. He looked around and saw nothing. He was alone for the moment. He dug his hands into the cold, sticky slime. His fingers made contact with Eden. He wrapped his arms around her body. The slime was up to his elbows and was freezing. He pulled her out of the sack; as it broke apart in tiny gooey particles. She let out a loud gasp and opened her eyes. Her body shook violently as if being electrocuted.

"Eden, it's okay," he was saying, "it's me,Gary, I'm here now. Gary. I got you." He rubbed her shoulders as her face fell to his chest. She started to cry. He held her tightly and continued to rub her shoulders and arms, trying to warm her. He ran his fingers over her head and hair. She was soaking wet.

"What happened?" he asked. She shook her head. She tried to stand, but fell back down.

"Eden, can you speak?" Gary asked, helping her to her feet. He held her until she was able to stand properly.

"Yes," she said. "I was carried off by something. I fell asleep. Each time I awoke there was a plate of food. Then I would go back to sleep. I would often throw up. How did you find me?"

"Luck," he replied. "Or perhaps divine intervention."

"Where is my dad?" she asked. Gary looked at her through bloodshot eyes.

"I'm sorry Eden. It got him." He took her hand and they began back the way Gary had come. Gary heard a whipping sound, and then a moist substance wrapped around his ankle. It pulled him down onto the dirt and dragged him away from Eden. It was a tongue, and it belonged to The Frogman.

8.

The tongue was smooth, yet moist and sticky. It stretched out about twelve feet, and was dragging its captive closer to the pond. Gary was astonished to see the fabled creature face to face. The Frogman pulled him closer and closer as the tongue recoiled. Eden screamed frantically, bending to grab Gary by his arms. He felt his body being pulled in different directions, like a dog toy. But this tug of war was life and death. His backpack slid off his shoulders and into the mud. Eden's grip was slipping. Inch by inch, The Frogman gained ground. Out from the pond the cacophony of frogs sang forth. The sound burst a heavy dread into Eden's mind. It was as if the frogs were singing Taps, for a funeral. But this song was not to honor the fallen, the song was a lullaby of doom. She tugged harder as Gary yelled in anguish. Through clenched teeth he muttered, "Gun! Backpack!"

Eden dropped his hands. This sped his pace closer to The Frogman. The creature dropped on all fours. His back legs bent backwards, then suddenly he soared into the air, hopping in their direction. His long tongue still wrapped around Gary's ankle. The Frogman's legs, long and muscular, extended, blocking the sun. His shadow covered Gary, who cried in terror as the creature was upon him. He felt his legs go deep into The Frogman's gaping mouth, his saliva drenching Gary. The spit was thick as honey and just as sticky. Gary saw The Frogman's eyes roll deep into the back of his head. He was now up to his chest in The Frogman's mouth. He could almost touch the vocal sack. Then a loud bang pierced the circumference of Chorus Pond. Gary's ears rang, but he watched as his captor's head exploded. Half of The Frogman's face dispatched from the rest of the head and flew through the air, splashing into the pond. Eden fired another shot and a bullet ripped through his chest, sending him backwards. Then a third bullet flew over him as he fell to the muddy shore. A black murky flow of blood drizzled out of The Frogman's corpse.

"Damn, you're a fantastic shot!" cried Gary. He was still half inside the mouth. The gooey saliva contained him. He tried pulling himself out of the mouth, but the tongue was still wrapped around his ankle. Finally free of the orifice he said, "Eden, shoot this damn tongue and let's get the fuck out of here!" Eden stood over him and shot her target dead on. Gary got to his knees. His heart raced like a gerbil on a wheel. Eden placed a hand on his shoulder. His eyes were bright with fright. Hers narrowed to comfort. She placed her forehead on his. "It's okay," she said. "Thank you for coming for me." He could have kissed her right there, at that precise moment. But he knew that would be cliché and more than anything they both wanted to be back in town. They scurried away from Chorus Pond. Back at the cabin Gary started his dirt bike and she entered her father's cabin. Despair clenched her heart in a tight death grip. She knew the Keeper of the Pond was responsible, but who would believe that? Grabbing her suitcase, she saw herself in the mirror. Her body was different, her physique changed. They rode to town in solemn silence.

9.

Detective Mumford sat with his legs crossed and a notepad in his hairy hands. He used his other ape-like hand to push his glasses back up on his nose. He scribbled all of Eden's and Gary's responses in the tiny booklet. But he still managed to laugh in his mind. Maybe Gary had Eden captive the whole time. Maybe this boy was who impregnated her. Most likely this fantastical story of a creature was all a cover up for the rapist that Gary had to be. Either way, Mumford sat with the two of them in the patient room of the Women's Clinic. Two days ago Eden had phoned Gary, telling him of her assumptions of pregnancy. He agreed to go with her to the clinic. Mumford was lucky enough to be questioning Gary the same day as the phone call. If it was Gary's baby, he would arrest him right then and there. Eden sat across from Mumford. Her face was grey as the moon. Her eyes were stained red from crying. Gary held her hands. He was quiet. She lowered her gaze to the shiny white tile.

"I want it out of me," she said, "fucking kill it."

"It's evidence, Eden," said Mumford. "I have to know whose it is."

“We told you!” Eden shouted. “Go to the pond; you’ll find the body!”

Mumford shook his head. He imagined that both of them were in cahoots. He was a five year detective, and had seen things that men would do. But also women. No more were women the princesses in distress; some of them were just as diabolical as men. He had once been on a case where a woman was having an affair. She had talked her partner into murdering her husband, together, as an act of sealing their love. They had decapitated the poor bastard and stuck his penis in the lifeless head. What pushed people to do this, Mumford would never know, but surely he would be there to put them away. The door of the room swung open, after a brief knock. Dr. Wan entered. He was a slim Asian man, very polite, very intuitive. But his eyes seemed as if they held back distress. He placed a hand on Eden’s shoulder.

“There are anomalies with your ultrasound. You are going to have triplets. However they are not forming the way they should be at this stage. Their cranial features are very abnormal and so are the toes and hands. They’re webbed. Their legs are long and slender. The spine is shorter than what it needs to be. Frankly, it resembles a frog,” he choked a little at the end of that sentence. He saw Eden’s eyes widen in astonished terror. She latched onto Gary’s arm, squeezing it for comfort. The doctor continued:

“It’s nothing like I have ever seen before. They should be about three inches by now, but all three are significantly smaller. I can’t seem to locate a sex organ at the minute and”- he tried, but Eden broke out in a hysterical rage of tears. Gary hugged her to no avail. Mumford jumped from his seat and left the room for some air. But as he did, he heard Gary ask about an abortion.

10.

The drive out to Chorus Pond was a fast one. Mumford knew he was short on precious time. Despite the hunger pains in his stomach, he wanted to see if he could recover the body of the creature. Then perhaps he would get a pizza. Before leaving the Women's Clinic entirely, he had seen the actual pictures of the ultrasound. There was no denying Dr. Wan's claims. His cruiser roared into the front yard of the cabin. Mumford leaped out of the car and ran towards where Gary had said he found Eden. Nobody believed the kid's stories. Sure the house was used as evidence, but nobody had gone to where Gary said to look, or believed what Eden had to say once she got to talking about a humanoid frog. He batted and tramped through the bushes and aspens. The air was cold and orange. The sun would set in about half an hour. He hoped to see something, something besides an ultrasound to prove Gary's innocence. But what then if there was a body? He could not take into custody a corpse. He prayed to God that Eden would get an abortion even if the Almighty's law might forbid it.

He finally made it to the shore of Chorus Pond. It was beautiful beneath the sunset. Tiny ripples rolled on the glassy surface. The orange-streaked sky, was mirrored in the water as the sun was descending. Mumford stood in the mud watching as a shadowy figure moved into the pond. He brought a hairy finger to his eyes and wiped tears away. Hundreds of frogs stared back at him, as the sun set behind the animals. They stood in a group. The frogs in the center held something on their backs. A figure that looked like a mutated man. With this creature stationed on their backs, the frogs disappeared beneath the watery surface into the depths. But just before the body was entirely submerged, Mumford saw that half of its skull was missing. Now he would have to inform his boss. Now this was a bigger discovery than any case he had been on. He trekked back to his police car. As he sat with his hand on his radio, he didn't know if he could eat a pizza after all.

The Pizza Boy

Let food be thy medicine and medicine be thy food. - Hippocrates

1.

Her apartment was peppered with drawings of her cat, George, and full of the harmonic tunes of Queen. Every single inch of wall space was covered in depictions of the orange, cream colored feline. He lay on the couch, watching his master paint away on her easel. Secretly in cat language, he judged her capabilities of getting his smashed in face perfect. Dani Mendoza sang along with Freddie Mercury as he hammered out "I Want to Break Free." She loved *The Works* album. But she also enjoyed *A Day at the Races.* Dani paused painting for a moment and gazed at George. What a fat, fluffy cat he was. She smiled.

"Now, you know, Mr. George, I really should be working on my sign for the march in two days. Emily is not going to like it if I don't get it done." George replied with a yawn, and a defiant look in his brown eyes. They stared at each other for a little while longer until finally he meowed in approval. Dani nodded her head and swept her eyes away from her pet. They peered over to some of her other drawings on her walls. Those were the ones that she had painted of *The Dark One.*

Her gaze bore into the paper, hanging on a wire with clothes pins. She doodled the drawing using only neutral colors. The face was a darkening grey, with round oval eyes, that were so black, eternity could be lost in them. The mouth snarled into an orifice of gnashing doom. The skull structure abnormally enlarged. Bony skeletal like fingers...

No! She mustn't think of those things. *The Dark One* who had terrorized her one month prior. Suddenly her cellphone rang. George ignored the wailing device and Dani jumped in fright. She got up from her stool and snatched her phone off the kitchen counter. It was Emily. Her girlfriend. She paused her music and answered the call.

"Hello, babe," she said. It felt good to talk to her. Especially when she was about to cry. A fear had started to bubble up inside of Dani, but hearing her girlfriend's voice calmed her. It had been a delightful six months so far, and she hoped that they had many more ahead of them.

"How was work today?" asked Emily.

"Well, besides the stupid bitches I work with, it went okay. Maybe I can start hustling some more paintings of George. Just got to find people that like Persian cats."

"You serve enough people coffee, maybe slip a drawing or two on a napkin with them," said Emily. "How's the sign coming along?"

Dani hesitated. Here she goes with all the questions. Why did she always want to know everything? Dani cared for her, but hated when her bossiness and demanding attitude reared its ugly head. "It's going okay," answered Dani. "You haven't started yet, have you," said Emily. "I know you're barely getting over your accident. But you have to try. Nothing gets better without trying. Nothing gets done without trying. Trying equals doing. I was scared too. That night you crashed your jeep in the woods. You were out there for a whole night. Lost."

Dani took her cellphone away from her ear. George sensed her uneasiness and climbed into her lap. She petted his furry body as tears fell from her chin onto him. He stretched his neck out to her, trying to cheer his master up. Finally she put the phone back to her head.

"You were not there. You don't know what I saw, what I felt." she said.

"You've told me hon, and I've seen your drawings. *The Dark One,"* said Emily.

"No! You don't speak his name," Dani shouted. "The bright lights, the fingers! The pain!"

"They found you lying about eight hundred feet from the accident. Yes, you were naked. Yes you had a weird tan on your body. You were hallucinating! Fingers? You weren't even touched!"

"No, stop it!" cried Dani. "You don't know! I can't sleep, I dream of that horrible, disgusting face."

Emily sighed into the phone. A long, heavy breath pushed its way into Dani's ears. She was crying now. Emily felt bad, but also knew that Dani needed to be tough. Emily thought this over in her head. "Remember how we met at a rally? The one for Planned Parenthood?"

"Yes," replied Dani. "You were so beautiful and strong."

"Remember all the love that was felt?" asked Emily. "How men, women, and children came together to show support of the organization. How I was shunned at first, for stating that the Parenthood had been developed and funded by eugenics? But then I showed them that they offer more than just abortions. How we need contraceptives and birth control. How women in undeveloped communities or struggling in the ghettos need those things? They needed clinics and medicines. And you were there with your sign. The one that said: "anything you can do I can do bleeding"."

Dani chuckled. "At least I didn't have a pussy on my head."

Emily laughed. "You are so capable of anything you want. You can overcome this fear. This face that haunts you. Together there is strength. I am here for you, okay." Dani looked down at George who was purring faster than the speed of light, and sounded like a motorboat sailing down a lake.

"Okay babe, I'll get back to it. See you tomorrow at the movies." Dani hung up the phone. George purred louder and louder as she sat there petting him; contemplating that horrible night one month ago. The time she met *The Dark One.*

2.

It was August last month, the summer was hot and stingy. But in Oregon it was bearable compared to other parts of the country. Dani was stoned, and driving home from the annual coffee camp weekend. Her boss made it mandatory that once a year they all go up to Trout Creek, to smoke out and drink beer. August sixth was coming to an end as she sped down the 395 back to Burns, Oregon. She was in the middle of the Malheur National Forest. It was eight at night, and Dani had not heard from Emily in two days. Dani loved the forest, but no service on her phone made it hard to endure. Her phone was an extension of her, an extra body part if you will. She really liked Emily and wanted to tell her she'd be home in time for them to hang out.

Dani took out her cellphone and started to text. She lowered her eyes from the road. A car honked. She swerved; she had drifted off into the oncoming lane. A commercial truck blared its horn, as it flew past her. She returned to the correct lane of travel, and dropped her eyes back to her phone's screen. This action set into motion the night that would change her life forever.

A doe came prancing out from the forest. Without warning, the deer leaped out merrily onto the highway. Before she could maneuver out of the way, Dani hit the animal hard, knocking it to the asphalt. She felt the jeep glide up and over the poor dying creature. With a force, she over corrected, jerking off into the woods. The maple and red alder trees swirled by in a leafy jumbled bouquet of haze. She tumbled down a hill and smashed into a great Oregon White Oak. The chaos of the crash finally came to a rest.

Dani opened her eyes and saw she had her face in the airbag. She tore it away, realizing she could move her arms. Her left leg seemed to be stuck as her door was crushed inward. The windshield was busted, but she remembered she had removed the top of her jeep prior to the camping trip. She looked around for her phone. When she couldn't locate it, she figured it must have flown out. Her seatbelt was carved into her neck. She unbuckled herself. She was able jiggle her left leg a little and managed it out of its confines. She opened the glovebox and found her flashlight.

She started her assent to the roof of the vehicle. She cursed herself for being so stupid. There was no reason to text; simply a call would have sufficed. Or perhaps it was all a big mistake in the first place, coming out here with all these losers just because her boss said it was mandatory. She could have called in sick or thought of some excuse to exclude herself from this trip. But time does not rewind, and now she had to get out of there to a hospital. Her leg was getting worse as she fumbled around in the dark. She limped around her jeep, and found her First Aid kit scattered about. Dani decided it was useless to try to locate its contents in the dark.

The beam extending from the flashlight bounced around the shadows. She tried to remember in which direction was the hill. She had slid pretty far away from it. Finally her beam caught a trail of broken tree branches and battered bushes. She started that way, ducking under timber limbs and striding through tall grass. Almost reaching the base of the hill, her leg locked on her. All the pain of a stab, jolted into her leg and thigh. It felt as if a thousand pins or swords had stuck her. She fell to the ground, crying out. Dani took deep breaths and started to crawl towards the hill. An owl hooted nearby and bushes rustled elsewhere. Her mind was spooked and body raging with panic. She reached the bottom of the hill and realized she could not climb it. Not even if her leg had the strength of Donna Moore. The hill had actually been a cliff. The jagged edges mocked her. She rubbed her leg trying to soothe the pain. Her hair clung to her head like a nest of snakes. The sweat and blood mingled in it, gave it new density and weight. She touched the top of her head and found a gash was there. She felt the blood run down the nape of her neck.

Dani crawled faster. Now panic swept through her body at a rapid pace. Her heart ticked faster than it ever had. Her mind played different scenarios to this nightmare. A bear would come along and kill her, or a cougar would eat her. Or simply a snakebite, or maybe she'd just die of hyperventilation and dehydration. She crawled around in the dark, with only the low yellow beam to guide her through this darkening stage. She wondered if her curtain would be down soon. She cried out to the sky, "If you're up there, help me! You hear me? You fucking help me! Is this punishment? Is it!"

A rumbling sound came from above the forest. The clamor was grand; it resembled that of a plane. It was a hum of great magnitude. A force of wind swirled around where Dani lay. An excruciating light shone down from the heavens. It instantly burned her clothes off her body and she felt herself start to levitate. Then a body dropped from the light. Its scorching beam lowered the being onto Dani. Its skin was tight and leather looking. The head abnormally large with a narrow nose cavity. The neck was long and skinny. The eyes resting in its skull were blacker than any starless sky. It grabbed her with a firm, bony hand that had three digits only. Its mouth spread into a gaping hole. She felt like her spirit was being sucked from her, when from out of the illuminated beam a wild animal leaped onto her attacker. Then another joined him. They were two Lynx cats and they scratched, tore, and bit at the invader. Their tailless bodies bobbed in the shadows, fighting with the strange phenomenon from the sky. She fell back to the ground and rolled out from under the dress of light. The wild cats were rising into the sky now, with their dinner holding onto them instead.

The invader held the wild cats, one in each hand. Then suddenly all went white and she fell asleep.

She awoke in the back of an ambulance sometime later. She would need stiches in the back of her head and physical therapy for her leg. Two of her toes were fractured. She guessed she was lucky. But she knew what she saw. *The Dark One* still called her from somewhere in the stars.

3.

A rapping on her apartment door brought her back to present time. The knock was abrupt. It startled her, and George leapt from her lap. He retreated underneath the sofa. Dani reached for her robe, and hurried across her living room, feeling the soft carpet swell between her nude toes. She paused her music, and reached the door, spying out through the peephole. It was a delivery boy. He held a pizza in his hands. Dani opened the door, leaving the chain lock intact. She peered at him between the slit in the door. He had dirty-blonde hair and kind, blue eyes. He seemed to be about her age and awfully skinny. Her visitor sported a grey polo shirt with no logo and black denim pants. His name tag read Dustin, but there was no logo or company name engraved there. "I didn't order any pizza," replied Dani. She scowled at him, trying to figure out his motive.

"Is this 1395, west Elm Street?" he asked. "Apartment 123?"

"Yes."

"Well," he said, "I have a large pepperoni with pineapple for this address."

There were certain things in life that were coincidence or luck, and sometimes just plain weird. How was it that he would show up with her favorite pizza pie, when she knew clearly she did not order one? He stood before her, perfectly still, behind the door. His deep aqua irises continued to stare into her.

"It's already been paid for," he said.

"Really?" asked Dani, with astonishment. She could feel this brief interaction becoming stranger.

"Yes ma'am," he stated, "by phone." He shifted his weight and switched hands with the pizza. "Now if I show back up with it, it comes out of my paycheck. I would throw it away, but I don't believe in wasting food."

Dani stared back into those beautiful mesmerizing eyes. They seemed to glow of shiny diamonds. The aroma of the pizza with its melted cheese, and layered tomato sauce floated into her. It was the greasiest of all pies, but was the heaven her stomach now demanded to have. Against her better judgement and warnings within her heart, she unlatched the door. It was as if a veil had been spread over her feminist ideals, eradicating any core sense within her. It seemed that the scent was so intoxicating that it hindered her, casting illusions within her mind. She smiled at him. She remembered she had some dollar bills in her purse. She opened the door all the way for him.

"Okay," she said. "Come on in, while I get you your tip."

"Thank you," replied Dustin. He walked inside Apartment 123.

4.

When pizza boy, Dustin, stepped over the threshold and into her home, Dani realized how tall he was. He towered at least six feet, with a few inches to spare. He stood in her living room while she ventured into the kitchen to locate her purse. George yowled a disapproving octave from beneath the couch.

"What company are you from?" called Dani from the kitchen.

"Ares," Dustin answered. He started to walk around the room.

"Never heard of them," she said.

"We're pretty new," he said, as he looked into a picture resting on the coffee table. The picture was of Dani, with another girl. "We believe in pure ingredients, which is better quality. That is how our bodies survive, is it not?"

Dani did not reply to him. He figured that was alright. Not many people understood what it meant to ensure the survival of their race, or the steps necessary to reach that point. He put the picture back on the coffee table and looked up. He saw Dani's many drawings of the hissing feline beneath the couch. He also noticed the darker ones.

"I really like your drawings," Dustin remarked, as Dani returned to the living room with his tip. She smiled again at him, feeling bewildered for doing so. He placed the pizza next to the picture he had been studying.

"Which ones?" she asked, handing him the money.

"Those," he pointed to the dark earth tone colored drawings. "The scary ones."

"Really?" asked Dani.

"Truly," he responded, "you have a great talent."

Her smiled faded away. Her mouth and eyebrows turned into a frown. George hissed and spit from his hiding place. They were mean, nasty sounds. Dani ignored her pet, savoring the aroma of the pizza. Once again her senses became scrambled. Both parties stood there staring into each other. Finally Dani shook her head and said, "I don't want to talk about those."

"Do you sell them?" asked Dustin, not getting the hint to leave the apartment. He wore a smile that seemed to illuminate his face, brightening the whole apartment. Dani scowled but the smell of the food engulfed her. "Which one?" she asked.

"Surprise me."

Feeling strangely unusual, she looked him over for a final time. Judging this weird conversation and boy. She did need the money and her stomach was roaring. She turned away from him, her back facing her visitor, as she bent for her stool. George fluffed up into a hairy ball of anger under the couch. But Dani was too focused on her artwork to notice what was transpiring behind her. George watched in terror as the pizza boy started to transform.

If George had been a human instead of a feline animal, perhaps he could have warned Dani. He spat, hissed, and yowled godawful cries from his refuge underneath the sofa. The aroma was so dense now, it saturated the entire home, and all of Dani's senses were gone. She did not see Dustin start to rip the flesh from his own face.

Dustin grabbed the sides of his skull and started to pull. A line emerged down the center of his face, arching over his nose, through his mouth; down to his chin. The skin pulled freely apart without restraint. The flesh continued to split, as new skin emerged. The new texture was smooth yet rubbery and a fishy grey. Dustin stepped out of his old discarded skin suit and snuck up on Dani standing on her stool.

She turned, meeting Dustin face to face. But what was once Dustin, now showed no trace of the pizza boy. A horrible deafening scream emitted from her throat. The drawing she had chosen for him, dropped from her hands and floated to the floor. It was the drawing of the very same creature that stood before her now. His rubbery three finger hand seized her by the neck, uprooting her from her stool. The new black, inky pupils pierced her, glared at her. His jaw dropped into a long gaping hole. He inhaled and she could feel her spirit start to drain from within her. He sucked harder, her spirit leaving her body in a paralyzing pull. After her energy had been drained, her carcass fell to the apartment floor. The last thing her conscious mind beheld was a vast ocean of oily waves, where she sank into an eternal black abyss.

5.

George slowly surfaced from underneath the living room couch. He lowered his head as he ran towards who used to be his master. Dani lay there motionless, the cat curled up next to her. Her spirit was long gone, captured by *The Dark One.*

The Dark One stepped back into his old skin. He pulled it up over his alien body like a firefighter putting on his suit. When the flesh met together on his face, tiny skin limbs stretched and absorbed one another sealing his disguise. He looked down at George. The animal spat and hissed, baring its pointy teeth. He could kill this miserable pet, but decided to let it be. He switched back on *Queen. Bohemian Rhapsody* blared into the confines of Apartment 123. He opened the apartment's door and left George listening to Freddie, while mourning over the dead body.

In the disguise of Dustin, *The Dark One* sat in his Ford Ranger. He had two more pizzas resting on the passenger seat beside him. He reached for the glovebox and popped it open. An hour glass jar was nestled inside. He took it out, and the contents inside glowed a white wispy hue. The white turned into an azure fog. He opened the jar and placed his mouth over the exposed top. He exhaled. A faint snowy shadow blew into the jar. He slammed the lid closed, making sure her spirit would not flee. Dustin placed the jar back into the glove box. He started the truck and turned back onto Elm Street. The night was still fresh. With only two more deliveries to go, it wouldn't be long until he could leave this planet. It was always with the right ingredients, never anything less. The jar of souls was almost full.

6.

After the final two souls were collected, he left the town behind him. He raced the Ford Ranger down the 395 at massive speed. The road signs were a blur to him, but that was alright. He did not use them. He knew exactly where his pickup point was. It was time to leave the planet until next month. He enjoyed leaving. He thought the species here were disgusting. Only a few were refined. But some of the best quality food had weird ingredients. He knew that sometimes even if it was good, if you could tinker or change it slightly, it could be even better. He turned off the main road and sailed through an endless ocean of trees. The forest rushed past him in a cosmic swirl of foliage. *The Dark One* entered a clearing where he parked the truck directly in the middle. Suddenly his radio blared and came to life, the dial switching stations in a cacophony of twisted guitars and talk shows. An illuminating light crashed upon him. So bright, he could not see. The vehicle started to rise off the dirt. It climbed higher into the sky with its driver.

The Dark One rose swiftly into the midnight sky. The destination was the spaceship which continued to pull him upward. The truck along with the driver, finally came to rest as it was sucked into the bottom of the ship. Dustin smiled. It had been another great delivery day. He opened the vehicle door and stepped out into immense darkness. When his foot hit the floor, a glow expanded, brightening the docking bay he was now in.

Five other cars were sitting in the bay on either side of his transport. They also had gone out on deliveries. Many places, different areas, all with the goal of obtaining souls. He held his jar as he departed out from the docking area. He stood in an elevator that started to spray a light mist upon him. His human skin disintegrated and he was now back in his natural form, *The Dark One.* The elevator paused, he exited, heading towards the feeding chambers.

He walked casually as he passed the many rooms lining the hallway. The walls were transparent and he could see his other shipmates going about their duties and activities. In passing they greeted him, not by words but subliminally. A small voice popped into his head in his native language of clicks. A sound, much like the voice of a dolphin. There was too much work to be done; talking would only take up precious time. The others on the opposite of the hallway worked on the ship or performed operations on captured species.

These prisoners consisted of other aliens, few humans, and other various life forms. All work was to be completed by the time they reached their home planet of Ares. The red planet was their home and salvation. He sent a greeting back telepathically and continued on with his jar of souls. It was feeding time.

7.

He came to the feeding chambers. The ship's doors were bubbly portals that spun in a starry clockwise motion. Holding tightly to his jar, *The Dark One* stepped into the room. Here stationed on the walls were various rows and rows of jelly sacks that served as incubators. These apparatuses housed the ship's offspring. In the middle of the chamber was an egg-shaped container, its matter constructed of the very same material as the ship. Here he was familiar. This is where all his species had been created. Where he had been educated; birthed into eternal space and time. He stood over the egg. Using one of his pointy fingers he smashed away on the keyboard hooked up to the egg.

Slowly the top rose off revealing the same azure fog, which began to float around the lid. The fog turned dense as shadowy human fingers and hands grasped at the air. Their attempt was futile, their souls dying. *The Dark One* twisted the lid on his jar, opening it. With his three fingers he tilted and poured the contents of his jar into the egg. Now the offspring would feed and grow strong. He watched in honor and pride as the very last misty soul dripped out of his jar. He stamped away on the keyboard, closing the lid.

He was successful once again on finding the right ingredients. *The Dark One* laughed a gibberish guffaw and headed to his sleeping quarters. In another month he would return to Earth. He already knew his coordinates. Except this time he would be what the humans call a *Bartender.* They would all drink 'til death.

The Tavern

There be those who say that things and places have souls, and there be those who say they have not; I dare not say, myself, but I will tell of the street. – H.P. Lovecraft

1.

Donnie's used to be a nice tavern. It was in desperate need of renovation, but I loved this shithole. It would appear that I love alcohol and the stench of the joint, but in fact I sit my thirty-two year old ass down on this stool, because I have found love. I wish I could say that it was located at the bottom of every glass I finished, my joy of the pool table and its colorful balls, or the piano that sits in the corner of the tavern. But that would in fact be a lie. Maybe that would be alright, since lying is what we do best. We barflies sit here in a tinted shadow, sucking up our sweet dung, booze. We feed on it, need it; lie to ourselves that we wouldn't be complete without it. There I sat on this ratty old stool mesmerized by the bartender, Harley. It wasn't just her deep, penetrating, green eyes which sat behind thick-rimmed glasses that stirred my heart; nor was it her wavy jet black hair, or those little white pearly teeth that clicked together when she spoke. It was her heart and kindness that shone through. Whenever some filthy bum would waddle in, strung out on some type of drug or mumbling some profanity or urinating in the corner, she would show them love. She gave them water, food, and sent them on their way. Sure, Harley's body was that of angel (she never wore a bra) but that didn't bother me. I understood that she worked it for a living. Every guy there knew she was off limits. Some outsiders would try, but we regulars always protected her.

Locals, what a thing of the past. It's only me and Skinny Tim now. The elders have all passed, the younglings don't like the gloom caliber of the tavern, and the middle men like me, are all stuck in deadbeat marriages. I do not tell you this in vain, for I only aim to express my desire for Harley Dean. I wasted two years trying to muster enough courage in my bones to tell her how I felt. I didn't want to be a lapdog or a stray, so I became the roaming mutt that she fed booze to. The juice helped ease my pain of revelation that my old ass would never be the love interest of a twenty-four-year-

old girl. But every Christmas and birthday, I was there to give her a gift.

The tale of which I write began on October, the thirty-first. That's right, Halloween. Donnie's ain't that packed, but we're still shoulder to shoulder like sardines in a can. I retired from my eight-to-five slaving, and sat on my same blown out stool. Skinny Tim stumbles over, already lost in a sea of booze and mumbles the words out to me, "Aye Scotty! What's good, my man?"

I look at his pointy body that reminds me of a utensil to clean my ears, and I nod in the most fashionable way. "Hey Skinny Tim, same old shit. But Harley here, she makes every holiday special." I feel awkward for saying that. But why should I? Two years is a long time not to tell someone your feelings. Especially if those feelings are expanding like helium in a balloon almost ready to pop. Harley smiles at me from across her bar top. She's cleaning a couple glasses and then prepares a shot for the man in the tall brim hat. He stands back in the shadows surveying the place. He's been a regular for about a month now. I don't know his name, but I know he's alright.

Skinny Tim leans closer to me, I can almost taste the vomit and gin saturating his tongue. He puts a twig-like arm around my shoulders. I can feel his bones dig into my skin.

"Fucking nasty weather out. I hope Harley lets me sleep here tonight," he declares, and then proceeds to drink my Jameson mixed with Sprite, which is resting in front of me.

"Hell's wrong with you?" I demand as I snatch it from his pointy fingers. "That's mine!"

"I'll have what he's having, I'll be over there on the couch beneath the window." He places a twenty on the bar. "Keep the change, girl."

Skinny Tim gives me a final pat; his strength is all that of a bag of chips. He plops down below the huge oval glass window; its pane streaked with the tears of the sky. Thunder booms loudly as if God is laughing at this deluge. I gaze out the window, looking solemnly at the cemetery up on the hill. I always thought it was weird, having a bar located at the bottom of a graveyard. But this is Kony, Massachusetts; we're built on top of hundreds of bodies. Hell, the very road we drive upon is nothing but blood stained ground. I watch the water drip in abstract patterns down the glass, trying to grow a bigger set to tell Harley how I feel, when she startles me.

"Hey Scotty! Another blend of your favorite? Or something else?" she asks. Her voice so dreamy, it causes the caterpillars in my heart to skip the metamorphosis stage and go right to butterflies. I must have stared at her for more than a minute.

"Scotty, you okay?"

"Yes," I answer, locking my eyes into hers. "It is awful weather we're having. I'll go with another blend, dear."

She goes about her duty. I watch as she mixes my drink. Adding a double shot of Jameson, the way I like it. There is no lust here on my part. I would be fibbing if I didn't say I wanted to sleep with her. But not a cheap, boozed-up screw, it would be heartfelt and sincere. I already know what she's been doing all month. This is her favorite holiday season. Scary stories, pumpkins, the horror movies. Damn, how she loved those films. In celebration Harley would watch at least one or two horror movies a day, for the whole month of October. Now she places the glass on my coaster and takes my old one away. I long to be that cup in her hand, but I don't believe that would happen. She and I have never spent time together outside of Donnie's. She knows I am single, but never asks me about my affairs. Sometimes I ponder if that means I have a chance.

She watches me take a swig and then cheerfully returns to me. A huge smile is spread across her face like perfect butter on the perfect slice of bread. I return the smile with a bigger one of my own and ask, "What film did you watch today?"

Harley's eyes sparkle. She steps back from the counter and raises her arms. I laugh at what she's doing. Well, I am pretty buzzed now, but watching her raise her arms and make chainsaw noises is adorable. She continues her movements waiting for me to guess. I burp a little and wipe my mouth. "The original, or the remake?" I inquire.

"Aw darling, you know I love the originals." She belts out a long bellow of a chuckle.

"Yes," I say, "Tobe Hooper's vision was horrific in all the ways possible. But did you know the biggest secret about that film?"

"Yeah, Scotty, that it's not an actual tale of mutilation and macabre. There's no real Leatherface."

This time I laugh after I swallow a gulp of my drink. She's right. I know it, she knows it. We all know it. I place my glass back down. I rub the stubble on my chin. We keep grinning at each-other. I wonder what she's thinking.

"Do you know where he came up with the idea?" I ask.

"Yes, he was in line at a hardware store; he saw a rack of chainsaws and knew that was a faster route through the crowd to the register."

By then, it's all over. We are both laughing and hanging onto one another. It's beautiful to hear her laugh. The sound sends those butterflies throughout my entire body. Out from behind me, the tall brimmed hat man appears, placing an empty tall glass on the bar top.

"Another Stella please, hon," he says.

Harley stops laughing, trying to refine herself. She smiles at him and nods. He takes a seat down next to me. We acknowledge each other. He reeks of tobacco. His suit is very well groomed. He stares into me, I want to turn away, but something holds me there.

"Does anyone ever play that thing?" he asks of me, pointing in the direction of the piano. I shake my head. He frowns at this.

"My name is Bucky," he says, holding out his hand. I shake it and relay my name to him.

"Nice to meet you," I say.

"I came down here from Westfield on a job opportunity. But I guess they don't like my playing."

Harley returns with his beer. He takes a long dramatic drink. I decide to keep the conversation going. Skinny Tim can't be my only friend. If we're all barflies, might as well keep them coming.

"You're a musician?" I ask.

"Damn right. I used to play in New York City as a backstage artist. Then moved to Westfield because I got tired of the studio and the politics. I taught music, private lessons. Then the school here said they needed a music teacher. But I guess I'm too eccentric."

Bucky takes another long drink of his alcohol. I smile at him and wave Harley over to us. She came prancing over, eager and delighted to be included in our conversation. She stands before us. I nod to my stool neighbor.

"Is it okay if Bucky here plays that piano?" I ask her.

"Sure," she says, her eyes wide with wonder.

"Is it tuned?" asks Bucky.

"I believe so. Boss man was in here last week playing away on it. The music was pretty, so I assume it is. Always wondered why he kept it in here. Now I know why. He can actually play."

Thunder booms overhead as the sky splits apart. It rattles the glass in the windows and knocks at our hearts with a demanding pounding. Outside the rain spits at Donnie's as if to try and drown it. Bucky rises from his seat with his beer and a coaster. I see Skinny Tim watch this new fellow with a look of suspicion. I shake my head sideways and Skinny Tim nods. Everything is okay. Bucky sits on the piano bench and sets his coaster and beer down. He flips up the lid over the keys and smiles. He runs his fingers over the smooth wooden exterior of the instrument. He pops his fingers and stretches his arms. Then as if an apparition had gripped him, he begins to play a soothing melody. As I listen I start to realize the tune. It was "November Rain" by Gun's n Roses. Damn, I think to myself. Tonight has to be the night. This song reminds me so much of Harley. She peers over at me, lip-syncing the words.

She is awestruck at the beautiful music escaping from Bucky's finger tips. I sing the lyrics along in my head, and hope that maybe if I sing them aloud, she would hear me. But I shut that notion down, and turn away from her. I instead, resume my stare at the window behind Skinny Tim (who is now singing and swooning his head to the music) and drink the rest of my alcohol.

As my gaze is transfixed on the outside world of Donnie's, I start to notice something different. Something quite odd. What looks like objects of some sort, are racing down the cemetery hill without anyone behind them. The objects are rectangular and dark. Lightning flashes and I see them clearer. But I still can't make them out. They seem to be about six to eight feet long. I realize the hill is flooding. Which means the graveyard is flooded. With these two ideas floating in my head, I watch as they get closer, gaining speed. One corner of the cemetery is adjacent to the bar. It is at the tavern's exact height. This means that the buried are at exact level as myself and other barflies. The hill rises above Donnie's, so I start to wonder if we're going to flood, when suddenly the window above Skinny Tim shatters, exploding into a million shards. A coffin soars through the glass, landing directly into the back of Skinny Tim's head. His noggin is brutally shoved forward as the coffin plowed into it, decapitating him. Before I could even scream, five more coffins break into the side of Donnie's.

The wall buckles as the weight hits it, causing the roof to cave in. Terror erupts in my heart as I watch helplessly as the ceiling falls onto Harley. Bucky leaps from his bench as rain water gushes in. The coffins glide across the floor of the joint, helped by the propulsion of the water. The whole side of Donnie's is now creaking and tumbling as the water soaks it. The bitter wind cries in; the coffins knock over tables and crash into the bar top. I sprint over to Harley and hold her hands. She's alive, but stuck, the weight of the broken walls crushing her. Bucky is right by my side. The rain water starts to rise up to our ankles. He helps me toss the crumbled remains of the wall off her. But another coffin sails in, knocking into me and taking me rapidly away from them. I smash into the wall outside the bathroom. Another coffin hits the one pinning me, and now I'm trapped. I watch as Bucky gets Harley to her feet. A wave of relief washes over me. But then another coffin rams him, knocking him away from her as she falls onto the watery floor.

With what strength I have, I try to push the coffins away from me. They won't budge. I feel the flooding water rise up to my shins. I try to push again and one of the coffins breaks open. A disturbing stench reaches into my nostrils. The scent of decay and death. It's overwhelming and I begin to scream at Harley for help. She stumbles around the floating coffins, which by this point are like bumper cars, and tries for my direction. The ceiling splinters again, and plaster and beams break, falling directly into her path. A coffin takes her legs out from under her. I yell uncontrollably, screaming as if my voice would stop anymore of this hellish nightmare. There is a stabbing pain in my stomach. The weight of the coffin is piercing my gut. I feel like something inside of me has ruptured.

I can't see her now. The moldy death smell has engulfed me. The wind is cold and fierce as it whirls in. The coffins ram each other as Donnie's begins to fill up with water. The power blows and the darkness of a womb enters the tavern. Lightning flashes and I see Bucky trying to swim through the ever-rising depths of water. A few patrons are standing on tables. Bucky gets to the front door and pushes it open and the water starts to drain out, but more of the ceiling caves in on him.

2.

A year later and the bar is back up and opening tomorrow. I was happy to help with the renovations. Many men have ventured in and rebuilt the joint. It's quite lovely. They talk in hushed tones about how quickly they were able to get it accomplished. I always nod to them and speak, but they ignore me. Harley serves them drinks along with the new bartender, Susie. The two don't really get along, but that's alright because they work different shifts. I sleep a lot more now. So does Harley. She says it's hard to leave this place. I agree with her. It seems I am always there now. Bucky too. He often plays music while we work. The workmen scramble and rush the piano to stop him. I guess they don't like music as much as we do. The men often complain about the temperature being too cold in certain parts of the bar. They bitch about the lightbulbs too. I always tell them it's an old, dank joint, what do you expect? But they ignore me. That's fine. Tomorrow is opening day. Exactly one year after the incident. I can't wait.

Something weird transpires that day. Not a single person acknowledges me or Harley. The place is filled with two types of people. The first group is there to drink and to eat. The second are in a group of four and led by someone speaking about the past history of Donnie's. Hey, whatever the town can do to make a dollar, right? Bucky is there with us, and he's dressed so nicely. He bows before the people and takes a seat at the piano. The instrument has been roped off now and I can't understand why. Harley stands next to me. We both know that something is not right. Something feels different. She slides a glass of beer down the bar and one patron bolts up from his stool and rushes out of the pub.

I look into Harley's emerald eyes and then I realize a spark is missing. Something that used to hold my stare for hours, has now burned out. Her pupil resembles that of a burnt head on a match. I embrace her, I don't know why I do it, but it feels good to hug her. We never really spoke about that October night, and I doubt we ever will. It will be Christmas soon. I wonder what I'll get her.

We stand side by side, watching Bucky prepare his piece. He has been working on it for months, waiting for this special day. He grins at us. I discover something about him that I hadn't noticed before. He looks sickly. His epidermis is pale. His fingers hover over the white keys; his toes arching above the foot pedal. He clears his throat. What seemed like a decade passes until finally his phalanges dance mystically on the piano. Donnie's erupts into a chaotic mass of frightful cries.

3.

The hysteria is intense. People scramble and shove. Some fall to the floor and are trampled by others. Some don't run, but rush towards the piano, with their phones or cameras flashing and recording. Bucky finally stops playing, but most of the bar patrons have fled. The ones who remain search the piano, totally ignoring Bucky. I feel sick to my stomach and Harley starts to walk towards him. The lights flicker and the rest of the people run for the door. The next image that follows is one that I will hold in my mind forever.

As the last groups of patrons leave the joint, a man walks amongst them. The people do not see him, but as he walks past, he shoves them sideways, without even touching them. He was lanky and tall. Almost anorexic. He carries something in his hand. It is a human head. It is in fact his own head. The head of Skinny Tim.

I try to run, but my feet stay planted in the floor as if made of roots. Harley falls to the ground in shock. Bucky holds her by the arms and kneels with her. I believe what we were witnessing is a ghost. Skinny Tim did not even walk, he floated above the ground hovering in my direction. He motions for Bucky and Harley to accompany us at the bar. He places his head on the bar top and seats his corpse next me. My mouth must be hanging because he closes it for me. His fucking eyes blink in his detached head and when the others stand behind me, he speaks:

"Hello friends," he says. "Please do not be alarmed. I know you must be feeling confused and frightened. I am not a ghoul or demon. Those only come here if invited. But alas I am stuck here. Stuck here since that godawful night when the coffins came crashing in."

I stare in disbelief. A headless ghost is talking to us, and his actual decapitated head is blinking. Harley reaches for my hand and

I hold it. Bucky steps out from behind us and places a hand on Skinny Tim's shoulder.

"How can I do this?" he asks of Tim.

"You don't understand yet? You don't know why the people ignore you, or why you scared the shit out of them just now?" he says. We all shook our heads. A deep sense of despair starts to creep up my spine.

"We're all fucking dead! Harley, you drowned. You, Scotty, died of internal bleeding, and you, musician, died when the ceiling fell on you!"

I collapse off the stool. They stand over me in a circle. Once all beautiful faces, now grey and charcoal-like. But the only one I am staring at is her. Harley Dean. I reach up and try to wipe away the tears cascading down her ashy cheeks. Some fall and splash onto my face and chest. Well, it will be Christmas soon. I wonder what I am going to get her. I guess I have all eternity to find out.

Rise of the Engelmann

Don't let the past steal your present. This is the message of Christmas: We are never alone. – Taylor Caldwell

1.

Lone Pine Cemetery was in fact not very lonely. The cement gravestones reached far over the snowy, patchy sea, protruding like little islands. The small wooden name sign dangling on green metallic arms, swung to-and-fro as a brief gust of wind brushed over it. Clive McClain sat cross legged on one of the bare patches of earth, in front of a grave. Every month he would visit his grandfather and read the poems or stories he had written. Clive was not a famous or even known author, but his grandfather's dying wish was that he would use those fingers for typing, his brain for stories. Clive finished up his latest piece, a limerick about the holidays, and stood to his feet. He inserted his notebook into the left breast pocket of his jacket. The cold Colorado sun poured down on him. Sunset Falls was a tiny, but growing, town. Its location was great for tourists and young people. It lay only twenty-five miles from Denver. Out from behind one of the larger granite headstones, Eli Boone appeared. He held a bottle of Jack in his left hand and was walking rather irregularly. Clive smiled. They had become buds two years prior when they both landed a job for the Jingle Bell Trio Company. It wasn't actually the best job, but during the holidays it was fun. The job was sort of a rent-a-Santa. No career here, just Eli and Clive as elves, with John Reynolds, their boss, as Santa. At first the three had made appearances at the elementary and high school, but this year Sunset Falls had just built a small shopping plaza, where John had hoped the trio would appear. The place wasn't anything fancy or high end. It would contain stores like Footlocker, ACE Hardware, some local businesses and chain restaurants such as Red Robin or Applebee's. But even with these names on the roster, the space was dingy and small. The population of Sunset Falls was only around the sixty-thousand mark, but was expected to grow as some small towns do. It was the end of November. Everyone's rush to meet family for Thanksgiving; the smell of humbleness, was fading. No more was the aroma of thankfulness. The scent now would be of material desire and an urge to spend money on things they don't need for people who don't care. Tomorrow was December first, and it was opening day at Cedar Plaza. Clive took the bottle away from his friend and washed his gums with the alcohol. It burned, but felt pleasant. He looked down at his deceased family member's grave and waved, "See you again, Hugh."

Eli laughed a high girlish laugh. He almost fell down, but instead leaned on a tombstone. He had a wild look in his eye. The kind Clive knew too well, the look of an exciting idea. Excitement that led to awful things.

"How about in a few days we head down to Chorus Pond?" Eli asked, his eyes dazzling.

"All the way down to Frog Mountain?"

"Yes," he replied shifting his weight on a grave marker. "I've heard some crazy stories coming out from there. Things about a Frogman. The media sensation is nuts."

Clive stared at him. His disbelief showed behind his eyes. Eli spat onto the lush grass and cursed. He shook his head and took another long drink from the Jack Daniel bottle and threw the empty container across the graveyard. It echoed in a splintering pop as it broke upon a headstone. "You never want to have fun anymore! I mean we have a shovel and chainsaw in the truck. The vehicle can make it through any terrain," he said. He walked over to a wooden bench and sat down. A long sigh pushed from his lungs, exiting his lips.

"It's not that," Clive said, following him. "It takes a whole day to get there, and it's not one of the coolest places to go. They say the creature's dead. So who cares?" Clive sat down next to his drunken friend. He playfully punched him in the shoulder. "Come on, let's go get some more beer," he said. As he rose back to his feet, his pocket started to jingle. A song wailed out from his denim pants. He fished his cellphone out of his pocket. It was John.

Clive glanced over at Eli who was still seated on the bench, lighting a joint. He looked up from the weed and smiled. Clive pointed at his ringing cellphone and said, “It’s John, dude.” Eli took a puff and grinned again. He shrugged his shoulders.

“We were supposed to be cleaning the truck and van! Remember?” asked Clive.

Eli coughed a little, which turned into laughs. “We had all day, its five already. We’ll do it tomorrow. Just answer the damn phone,” he said. Clive sat back down next to Eli. He flashed him an angry look, which prompted Eli to laugh hysterically.

“Hello, John,” said Clive, answering the phone.

“Clive, there are two things I need answered from you,” his voice was stern, yet delicate. As if their boss were talking to children. Clive sensed this, but stayed respectful. After all, this man did pay him.

“Yes, boss?”

“Where are the truck and van?” inquired John. Clive sniffed and pulled his jacket hood over his head; it was getting colder.

“The van is at Eli’s, and we’re in the truck right now.”

“Doing what? Certainly not washing them I suppose.”

“Eating,” replied Clive.

“You two better start shaping up! Another thing, they want us at Cedar Plaza for opening day tomorrow. Just like I hoped. We have everything except a tree. Now, the owner of the plaza is very old fashioned. He repeatedly told me no fake trees. He wants everything to be as pure as can be.”

Clive coughed a little as the smoke from Eli's marijuana entered his nostrils. He cleared his throat. "But Hank's lot won't have any trees until the third."

"I know, Clive, just find me a tree! Meet me at the mall tomorrow morning," he yelled. "Nine sharp!" John ended the call.

2.

The wind howled a mighty cry, as it swept its icy touch into the graveyard. Clive shivered as he returned his phone to his pocket. It was getting later, and winter nights were nothing to be taken lightly. They still had a twenty-minute drive back into town from the cemetery. Eli stood up and stretched, the joint already completely consumed. He took out a comb from his leather jacket, and pulled the teeth through his hair. He looked over at his friend.

"What did shithead want?" he asked, returning the comb to his pocket.

"He says we have to find a live Christmas tree by tomorrow. The plaza wants us to do the Santa meet and greet."

Eli scowled. "Already? Hank's isn't even open yet. Didn't Cedar Plaza open already?"

"Sort of," said Clive. "They already had the ribbon ceremony, and only a select few were allowed in to shop."

"Oh," said Eli. "The special ones."

"Yeah, so tomorrow is for the peasants, like me and you."

The two friends started their way back to the truck. The wind continued to dance around them. The sign jingled noisily on its metal noose. Suddenly, Eli stopped in his tracks. He slapped his knee and began to laugh. His face turned a bright shade of red. Clive stared at him in confusion. He punched him in the chest. "What's so funny?" he demanded.

"Look around us!" Eli spun in circles with his arms spread. "So many trees, right here. Let's chop one down. Who cares?"

Clive laughed loudly, his eyes almost teary. He finally gained composure. He studied the trees around them. Many aspens were present, also spruce. Being a native of Colorado, he identified a rather infantile Engelmann Spruce. The eight foot tree was providing shade for one of the residents buried here. He started to walk that direction. Eli followed with a toothy smile. He caught up to Clive. "Want me to get the chainsaw?" he asked. Clive nodded his head. Eli darted out towards the truck. He ran faster than any drunk Clive had ever seen.

Eli returned with the chainsaw to find Clive inspecting the tree. It was full, very green and even had a few cones. He ran his hands over the purple, reddish-brown bark. He smiled. It was clean of beetles or damage. "The limbs are kind of skinny, don't you think?" asked Eli as he prepped the chainsaw.

"John wanted a tree; here it is. I don't think Pete Williams here minds," said Clive, indicating whose grave they were standing on. Another chill traveled up Clive's skin as they began their task. They had two hours before dark. It was strange enough to cut down a tree in a graveyard, but to be parading around in one at night, was something nightmares were made of. The kind where you sink deep into your sheets, as if a force were confining you there. The feeling of a hovering soul in the corner of your room, or a shadow extending its arm from inside your closet. Or perhaps a tingly cold hand snatches your foot dangling off the side of your bed. Clive tried his hardest not to picture such things. The pair high-fived as the Engelmann crashed to the cemetery floor. Together, with Eli at the bottom and Clive holding the top, they carried their freshly cut tree to the bed of the truck. Inside the bed they stored ropes and a very large metal box of assorted tools. Some sap had presented itself on Clive's fingers as he secured the plant to the truck. He tried wiping the residue off on the blades of grass he stood upon. Eli noticed some on his hands as well. He was carrying the chainsaw when he slipped and fell. The power tool arched in the air and he tried to grab it, the razor teeth cutting into his palm and fingers. He winced in pain, quickly drawing his extended arm back; watching the chainsaw hit the ground.

Clive who was already starting the truck, jumped out and ran to him. A thin deep cut made itself known in Eli's palm directly under his pinky to middle finger. His index finger had a nasty gash that was tainted with sap. Eli who was not a crier, but a curser, screamed obscenities that would make any Catholic do multiple Hail Mary's, or any Christian stay under the water longer at baptism, just to drown out the profanity. Clive helped his friend into the passenger seat of the truck. He grabbed the first aid kit from the center console. Eli laughed.

"I'm too crossfaded for this shit!" he declared, slapping the plastic box out of Clive's hands.

"Shit, Eli! Stop that, I'm trying to help you," replied Clive.

"Who are you, my daddy?" shouted Eli.

Clive slammed the truck door as hard as he could. He hated when Eli got like this. To Eli life was a big Monopoly game. You get dealt, you deal, you live, and you die. Take it all in stride for the price of an admission ticket. That admission was birth, none of us asked to be here, yet we all fight a struggle every day, and for what? Just to clock out at the end? Who really won the game? All we can do is play. Clive figured he would let that fucker bleed if Eli didn't want help. Or let Eli doctor himself up anyway. He picked up the chainsaw and threw it in the back of the old pickup. When he returned to the driver's seat, he was surprised to see Eli's hand bandaged and the young man asleep. Little did he know of the nightmare being watched behind his friend's eyelids. He pulled out of the graveyard as the sun said its goodbye to the occupants.

3.

Eli walked through what seemed like a cloud. His footsteps made no sound, and he could only hear himself breathing. Pillows of fog rolled around him, billowing around each other almost as if they were dancing. It was dark, but Eli could see. What his eyes saw was never-ending space. His feet continued to propel him onward, but the direction never changed; neither did the scenery. A nervous feeling began to invade his consciousness. He felt watched. He sped up his pace and still returned to the never-ending dark space. He turned back the way he came, and the end of that trail was the same. Everything the same: a thickening fog, a dark maroon shade of space, and himself. He ran and ran, but his travels always brought him back to the same point. He collapsed to his knees, trying to catch his breath. When his breathing returned to a normal state, his ears recognized footsteps. Out from the depths of the rolling fog, a man walked toward Eli. He was tall and clothed in a stained pea coat. His hair hug from his head in long skinny strands. His face was hidden; his teeth chattering together like those windup toys. He came to a pause a few feet from Eli, who now rose from the ground. The chattering started to calm to slower clicks.

"Who are you?" asked Eli, in a timid voice. The man laughed, his voice shrill, sounding like the scream of a bird. It could hardly be deciphered as a laugh, but Eli knew that it was. When the man stopped this infernal noise, he finally spoke.

“I am Pete. Pete Williams,” he hissed. “You will listen to me. Obey me,” he said. His voice sounding so similar to a snake’s hiss from cartoons, that Eli felt all the flesh on his bones, tingle with goosebumps. His heart beat faster than any cadence in a marching-band parade.

“I shot up the hospital in Denver, in ’93,” Pete said. “Shit, you were probably just a boy then. But hey, now you will be my undertaker so to speak. I know you have a rifle in your apartment. You’re on your way there now. You cut down my tree, awoke my spirit and by blood you have let me in. The sap has infected you. Now is the time to kill, kill for me, Eli. Prepare the already dying for their final burial. The final face to see, is the Angel of Death, who I willfully beseech to welcome thee.” Eli screamed in his sleep, startling Clive who came to a shaky stop in a parking spot of Eli’s apartment complex. The vehicle came to a rest next to their company’s van. Clive shook his friend, finally awaking him from his comatose-like sleep. Eli’s face was pouring with sweat, his eyes bulged and were full of fright. He threw open the door of the truck and stumbled out into the cold night. A few flakes of powder fell from the evening sky. A small flurry that would soon lead to heavier snowfall. Without a word and by himself, Eli picked up the tree from the bed and started to walk to his home. Clive got out and headed over to the van.

“Don’t unwrap it until tomorrow, keep the limbs tied and give it some water!” hollered Clive. But his friend did not turn around, or say goodbye; not even a wave. Clive got into the van. “Be there at nine!” he shouted, trying one more time to get his friend’s attention. But Eli was already gone. Lost on the side of the complex, in his own deep, disturbing thoughts.

4.

The Engelmann was propped in the corner of his living room in a bucket of water. Eli sat on his couch with his hands together under his chin, his elbows resting on his knees. He peered at the plant now occupying his home. Something unusual was attached to that tree. This much he knew: there was a presence here. This presence was not the Holiday Spirit, but a malevolent one. He felt as though the tree was staring back at him; he knew the plant was alive, but something else resided beneath the bark. The awful chattering of Pete Williams resounded inside his brain. He punched the side of his skull in a feeble attempt to make the noise go away. But the sound did not vanish. It became louder.

Eli jumped to his feet, knocking over the living room table. It crashed to the vinyl floor. He screamed. He had no idea why, but he was frustrated. It felt like his brain was ripping apart. As if his cerebrum was under siege, battling a horde of evil at Helm's Deep. But there would be no Gandalf or Aragorn to the rescue.

"What do you want?" he cried out. His living room became silent. So still, that it seemed as if time itself had stopped. Then out of the tree a force flew. An invisible rush that knocked him to his knees. When Eli stood, he now had a new driver. A new personality was giving orders. Eli had no control as he walked to his hall closet. He paused, gawking at the white four-paneled door before him. He knew deep inside that he should not open the closet. He knew what the new personality wanted. He slowly raised his left arm and felt his hand squeeze around the bronze knob.

He felt like the frog who danced too close on the edge of the pot. Here he was now, dancing a waltz right on the edge of fire. If he continued with this dance, he knew nothing but a torrent of torment lay ahead. He could hear the chattering rise louder in his head. He was overtaken; no use in fighting. This was what was dealt to him. He turned the knob over and the closet door creaked open.

Hanging there were coats. All kinds of different jackets. He spied the one he wanted: a long, ink-black pea coat. He snatched it off the clothes rod and pushed the other garments aside. Behind the clothing items, sitting in its case, was an AR-15. Ammunition boxes lay scattered next to the weapon. Bending inside, he grabbed the gun and returned to his sofa. It was time to clean and polish the weapon. The chatter, which now controlled him, continued well into the night.

5.

Cedar Plaza was an obtuse, dome-shaped building. Wearing his pointy brown shoes, green tights, and a jade vest, Clive walked across the snowy parking lot. He stood before the automatic glass doors, perplexed. The shape and design of the plaza bothered him. Its curvy structure was built around a courtyard. Clive decided that whoever had designed this building was dumb. It was Clive's non-expert opinion that a glass dome ceiling was ludicrous. (Not to mention the gap created by the oval hole of a ceiling.) Corey Shem stood on the opposite side of the glass doors. The security guard recognized Clive and opened the doors for the human elf. Clive passed through the doors, carrying bags full of candy and a Santa suit. He nodded towards Corey and continued into the plaza. The courtyard dazzled with Christmas lights and soft snow. Picnic tables, and benches littered the area. Bushes and small plants that could survive the snow glared back at Clive. Smack dab in the middle of this makeshift Central Park, was a homemade North Pole, complete with a cardboard workshop and village. The cardboard depicted reindeer and elves. Positioned before the tiny village was a large cherry, poufy chair. Here is where his boss, Reynolds, would sit. Here is where Clive would spend the remainder of his day, smiling giddily at children and putting them on Santa's lap.

Constricting this kiddy attraction were the eight stores. Painted in Christmas décor, their storefronts radiated brighter than the Northern Lights. Clive shook his head, scoffing and then realized something even more peculiar. To his bewilderment, the Engelmann was already standing behind Santa's chair. Clive was standing before the chair when John hurried out from behind the village. Clive recognized his boss, but not the man who followed him. He was dressed in an elegant suit, and the air seemed to turn golden around him. When the pair reached Clive, John Reynolds smiled.

"Clive, this is Mr. Collin West, owner of Cedar Plaza," he said. Clive stuck his hand out, and Mr. West shook it firmly.

"Nice to meet you, Clive," he replied.

"Pleasure's mine," responded Clive. "Thank you for including us in your holiday festivities."

Collin West smiled. His teeth so white, Clive wanted to shield his eyes from the glare. They were a ghostly shade; not a single touch of tarter or blemish. "It wouldn't be Christmas without Santa and his Elves," he said. "Besides, I didn't buy this land just to watch it fail. I have a lot of hope for this town."

Clive nodded, amazed at the man's teeth. He glanced over at his boss. John had an even pearlier grin stationed on his face. Clive knew John had the best poker face of them all. It was unbreakable. John placed his hands on Clive's shoulders, in an attempt to advert his attention. His boss pushed slightly, trying to break free from Mr. West.

"Well Mr. West, thank you for showing me around. I believe my associate and I will go prepare for the onslaught of children. If you need anything, just holler," said John, pushing Clive further away. "Thank you Mr. Reynolds," said Collin West, as he stepped away in the opposite direction.

"What was all that about?" asked Clive, as he sat the bags on Santa's throne. John looked out of breath. He chuckled. "You wouldn't believe how much corn is shoved up that man's ass," he said. Clive snickered. When his laughter subsided he asked, "Where is Eli?"

John Reynolds looked in the bags, double checking their contents. "He got here super early. Put the tree in the water, dressed it; been moving around here like Flash. I saw him talking to a few store owners, even Corey from security. He got our village up lickety-split. What'd the two of you do last night anyway? He's been acting strange."

Clive narrowed his eyes at his boss. "How do you mean?" Holding his suit at his chest, John pointed out into the courtyard. There was Eli, power walking in their direction. But his body language was different, almost expressionless. He seemed to be robotic.

"Looks like a damn Terminator," said Clive. His friend was carrying a box of wreaths. His speedy pace led him past the two men who were gawking. When he got closer Clive hurried to his side. "How's the hand, buddy?" he asked. His friend paid no attention to him. He simply walked right on by. John Reynolds stood confused next to Clive. He had already strapped on his fake curly beard. He placed a hand on his employee's shoulder. "What was all that about?" he asked. Clive continued to stare at Eli until he disappeared into one of the department stores. Something was not right. Something in the air had changed; Clive could sense it. Eli wasn't in uniform yet. He was wearing a pea coat. There was one hour before opening, and they still had plenty to do.

"Go get dressed, Mr. Reynolds," Clive told his boss. "I'll finish up here." John nodded his head. "Just make sure you put some sugar or Vodka in the tree water. We need it to last all month." He turned away from Clive and started his way to the bathrooms. He glanced up at the glass doors. Corey was there locking them. But a few eager faces had appeared on the glass. Soon the parking lot would be filled with customers and annoying children. Christmas was in the air. Time to put on a jolly face.

Out from the speakers of the ceiling, Jingle Bell Rock blared into the atmosphere. The numbing days of the holidays were here. Clive filled big plastic bowls full of chocolate and candy canes. After that he bought a Mountain Dew and poured it into the bowl of the Engelmann. As it filled, so did the confusion in his mind. Something was floating on this holiday tune. Notes, that he felt would lead somewhere to pain and suffering. If only he knew how much. To his surprise, the tree shook. The limbs vibrated as if it were alive. He knew it was a living thing, but this was different; this was strange. The bottle emptied and he threw it into a metallic trash container at the end of the village. He gazed at the tree, waiting for it to stir again. When it did not move, he went back to his tasks. Still some finishing touches to be done.

6.

Eli walked silently behind Corey. He followed the security guard back behind the hardware store, and into the long hallway corridors that conjoined each store. Eli was after Corey for two reasons. The first reason was to disarm the guard of his sidearm. The second being to relieve him of his keys. Eli heard them jingle with each step Corey took. Right now, Eli was weaponless. Earlier in the morning he had stashed his rifle under the table next to the front doors of the plaza. Housed on top of the table were many pamphlets on each store, or restaurant. Opening day coupons also rested here. But the concealment of his weapon was not these items, but the gingerbread-man table cloth that hung down off the table. Its draped brown material kept hidden the deadly secret.

He hoped the gun would be safe. He knew no one had seen him hide it there. He figured the statement about the early bird and the worm was true. He was about to feast on many worms. Eli knew that he was not totally naked of weapons or skill. The new personality was in him, upon his very mind, making it his house. His hands were now not Eli Boone's, but Pete William's. He felt what they were capable of, *knew* what power rested at his fingertips and palms.

They reached the end of the hallway. Corey stood before his office, oblivious to his pursuer. There was an exit door staring back at Eli from next to the security office. Eli knew it was an alley, which led to the parking lot and trashcans behind the food court. He wanted to flee, but the chatter in his mind held him now. The chatter was in control. Corey stuck his keys into the lock of his office and was suddenly pulled back from the door. A beefy arm wrapped around his neck, another took his armpits and pinned his swinging arms. He was stuck. He was dragged out through the exit door, his keys remaining in the lock.

The pair fell to the powered ground. It was freezing, but Corey had little time to react to this new temperature. He had lost his chance at recovery. His assailant snatched his baton off his belt and swung it down onto his face. Corey saw that it was Eli, but it was too late. His vision started to blur. He held out his arms in a feeble attempt to block the blows, but then he felt his skull crack. Little rivers of blood spread out down his face and cheeks. Then all feeling was gone. Corey had moved on. The blood became denser on the lumpy face. Finally Eli realized his prey had died and stopped the beating. He stood to his feet and ventured over to the exit door. He pulled it open, inspecting the hallway. It was vacant; this was good. He went back to Corey's body and sat him up. Small blotches of red stained the snow. Eli decided that it wasn't so bad. The only security personnel had just perished. He dragged the corpse back into the hallway of the plaza. He took it through the now unlocked office door. Once he was inside, he shut the door calmly.

After stuffing the deceased into the corner of the room, Eli inspected the office. A long keyboard stretched out beneath a wall of monitors and fifteen cameras. Two computers hummed at him from farther down the keyboard. On the right was a chair with wheels for feet and a tiny boxed fridge next to a desk. A mirror disguising the first aid kit hung above the desk. He peered back at his reflection. There were a few spots of drying blood on his face. This prompted him to look at his hands. Yes, they were absolutely covered in Corey's blood. He spied a roll of paper towels on top of the fridge. He threw open the door to the unit and to his joy found a gallon of water and glass bottles of Coke inside. Using the water and paper towels he tidied himself back up. After he completed this he turned his attention back to the cameras. The parking lot was swollen with eager shoppers. Eli grinned an evil smile.

"And all through the house, all the creatures were dead, except the mouse," he said. His driver was happy now, which made Eli happy. This was going to be a blood bath. He unplugged the security cameras. Using the bloody baton, he wreaked havoc on the computers and keyboard. He smashed every electric panel to pieces. The machines sparked and hissed. He pocketed the guard's keys and stashed Corey's pistol in the back of his pants. His coat hid the weapon perfectly. He glanced down at the desk, realizing something he hadn't before. He gazed at a clock that read 9:40. Twenty minutes until opening time. He walked back out, locking the security office behind him. He started back down the hallway when the bathroom door flung open, almost hitting him. It was Mr. Reynolds.

Startled at first, but quickly recovering, John blocked Eli from continuing down the hallway. "Where are you going?" he demanded in a stern voice. Eli looked at his boss with an expressionless face. "Why aren't you dressed?" Mr. Reynolds tried once more. Without moving and without any emotion, Eli finally spoke.

"Corey is handling some other business, so he wanted me to open up the doors for him." He shifted his weight. John pulled his fake snowy beard onto his chin. He frowned at Eli. The two stared at one another for a few seconds more. "Hurry the hell up then. Santa needs two Elves, not one," said John Reynolds, as he scurried off down the long hallway leaving his employee behind.

Eli went on down the hallway in a confident, solid step. He looked rigid, but the propulsion of his long legs carried him fast. Finally he made it back out into the courtyard and stood at the front of the plaza. He looked around, discreetly checking if his weapon was still in hiding. It was. A smirk formed on his lips. He pulled out his cellphone and checked the time: five minutes until opening. He peered from behind the heavy glass doors into the crowd of shoppers. The mass of people stood in a snake-like form. More than half of the people making up the snake-shaped line had their heads down, staring into their cellphones. From inside his mind where Pete Williams now resided, he could hear his new driver laugh. That damn-awful chatter started to rise. The sound turned into a deafening clamor until it came out of Eli's own mouth. His attached spirit used Eli's eyes to admire the flock before the kill. The electric devices engulfed the cattle, just like cud for their eyes, they chewed on every pixel their screens launched at them. Eli produced his own phone, but it wasn't to check any social media update or use the internet, but to check the time. It was one minute until opening. Why not let the flock in early? This was going to be easy. He opened the glass doors for the herd.

7.

The wave of eager shoppers flowed forth, spilling into the courtyard. The mob of people quickly separated, some splashing into the stores, others forming a line in front of Santa's Village. Clive smiled his usual soft grin at the children, their eyes full of wonder. Some of the littler ones pointed at Santa, asking if he was real. Clive glanced up. He saw Eli still at the front of the store. He was acting weird. His friend was watching every person that came in. It seemed as if he was counting them. John Reynolds started chuckling and ho-ho-ing, awakening Clive from his stare. He went to the first little boy in line. Clive guessed he was around six years old. The boy wore a Batman & Robin shirt. Clive grinned.

"Nice shirt," he said. "Batman was always my favorite. I prefer Keaton's take on the role though." The boy tilted his head in puzzlement. Clive took his eyes to the child's mom. She smiled at him. "For now he just watches the cartoon version," she said. Clive took his hand and led the small boy towards Santa Claus.

From afar, Eli watched his old companions greet and seat every child. John really was a convincing St. Nick. He checked his phone again for the time, twenty minutes had passed. The chatter began to rise; he knew it couldn't wait any longer. He stuck the keys back into the wall slot, locking the glass doors as they rolled shut. Swiftly he turned, ducking underneath the small side table. He pulled his AR-15 out; simultaneously removing a magazine from the inside of his pea coat, jamming it into the weapon. He cocked the rifle and calmly made his way into the crowd.

Clive held out his hand for another little girl. She had bright blue eyes that radiated a pure, innocent glow. She took his hand, all in smiles and joy. Together they walked towards Santa. Reaching the jolly fat man, just before picking her up to sit on his lap, the little girl looked into Clive's eyes one more time. But suddenly something was wrong. The blue faded and a look of agony twisted on her face. She collapsed into Clive's arms as he hit the floor. Instinct had told him to fall, but a whizzing noise flew past his ear. His left lobe sizzled with a burn. Loud clanging bangs echoed throughout the plaza. Looking up he saw Eli firing a rifle into the crowd. He watched in horror as the bullets struck the shoppers, blowing chunks out of them. The bullets ripped through the air, they hardly had time to react. None fell to the ground as Clive did, but instead ran in a frenzy. This panic led to their demise. Continually they were mowed down by Eli and his rifle.

Eli was emotionless. The black weapon vibrated within his hands. He didn't even feel his injury that had been bandaged. The gun now was an extension of his hands, of his fingers. Of *Pete Williams.* He aimed, firing holes into the store fronts, killing the patrons inside. He gained ground as he headed toward the village. Kids screamed, but were quickly shot down, their bodies leaving the ground as the force of the bullet struck their skulls. Eli loaded another clip.

Clive, still holding the girl, rolled over behind Santa's throne, where a very scared Mr. Reynolds was hiding. His red, cozy hat was absent, so was his white beard. Sweat beat down his face in strides. He glanced at the little girl. "She alright?" he asked. Clive looked at her and saw that she had taken a round to the shoulder. She was bleeding, and the white dress she wore was drenched in the nasty crimson stuff. Clive nodded. "But she needs to get to a hospital. Shit, we all need to get out of here." A few stray bullets ruptured the throne. All Clive could hear were screams and gun fire blazing throughout Cedar Plaza. He peeked out from the throne and saw Collin West emerge from the hardware store on Eli's right. Unbeknownst to Eli, Collin produced a hand gun from his hip and fired away. Clive watched in paralyzed amazement as Eli's brains exited the side of his skull. His body fell to the floor onto a dozen deceased shoppers. What happened next left Clive nearly breathless. The Engelmann shook, its needles fell to the tiled floor.

The branches grew thick and formed into longer limbs. They became solid almost resembling legs. Clive watched as the tree perched on these new limbs as if they were feet. Its tree stand and skirt hung below as it elevated itself on these new, branch-like legs. Then with a mighty thrust of another branch, the tree took a swing into John Reynolds. The limb entered his back, straight through his stomach. His bile, breakfast, and intestines spilt, as he was lifted from behind the throne. The tree tossed him out over the dying mob of humans. Clive screamed.

Collin West saw Clive running, holding a little girl in his arms. The pair were headed his way. He felt his jaw drop when he saw the Christmas Tree bounding behind them. It had acquired two solid trunk-like legs. The mass of these new appendages were solid branches. The tree's form now lumbered across the plaza, *running,* the two solid limbs acting as feet. The damn plant was alive. Some injured shoppers left the shoe store and were met with the Engelmann's extensions penetrating them. All three people took a branch straight to the throat. The trio hung on the branch like human ornaments as the tree continued to run. Finally they slipped off, but their heads remained pinned on the tree. They were almost upon Collin who was frozen in fear, when Clive felt something on his leg. He fell to the ground dropping the little girl. He looked back and saw a string of lights had wrapped themselves around his ankle. They hugged tighter, like a python constricting its dinner. He was pulled towards the Engelmann, bouncing and slamming against the corpses Eli had sent to the afterlife.

Collin stirred from his frozen stance and helped the little girl up. A couple survivors had reached the front of Cedar Plaza and were banging on the glass doors. A woman took the girl from him. "No," he said, "there's another exit behind the hardware store. It's an alley by the food court. Hurry, call the police!" Collin returned his attention to the tree and fired a shot. The bullet hit the string of lights, releasing Clive from its grasp. Clive rolled over and used a dead man as a shield, for the oncoming limb that struck him. He saw Collin run back into the hardware store with a woman carrying the blue eyed girl. Suddenly from the left of the tree, a limb stretched, grabbing the survivors by the entrance of the plaza. The branch wrapped its wooden arms around each person's middle.

The tree squeezed until their stomachs popped. The blood bathed the glass doors in scarlet splashes.

8.

Now Clive was in the long, shadow-lit hallway. Mr. West was a few steps ahead of him and the woman carrying the girl was farther up. The three ran fast, even though they could feel their muscles start to burn and cry beneath their skin. A crash was heard behind them. Clive turned, looking straight at the Engelmann. It was racing towards them in a haunting sprint. He had no idea how a tree was capable of such a thing. (Let alone that the chain of events had really happened.) It must have been a great bottle of Mountain Dew.

The woman kicked the exit door outward. She was met with a cold breeze. She spied her car off to the left. In her mind she counted this as a miracle. She reached her vehicle. She sat the girl on the hood and fished her keys out from her purse. She dropped them into the snow. Falling to her knees, she began a frantic search for them.

Clive suddenly felt a branch coil around his abdomen. Then instantly he was thrown into a door of the hallway. He slammed into it, jolting his body into unconsciousness. Before his eyes closed, he saw smashed computers and Corey stuck beneath shelving. He looked dead. The tree hustled past Clive. Its stand and skirt blowing in the breeze as it reached the snow.

The woman found the keys. Hurriedly she unlocked her Jeep Patriot. She swung the door open. Collin was now there holding the little girl. A long skinny limb took Collins legs out from under him. He dropped the girl to the powdery ground and was lifted into the air. The tree sent him sailing across the parking lot. He fell atop the asphalt feeling his legs break. He started to sob. There was no denying this emotion. A ghost tree had just flung him thirty feet, and a man had shot up his mall. He continued to cry until he passed out from exhaustion.

Clive opened his eyes. The security office ceiling looked down on him. His body begged for rest. His right side was bruised and hip inflamed with pain. The door was smashed, its hinge pins strewn across the room. Clive limped to the mirror cabinet and opened it. He found a bottle of rubbing alcohol. He maneuvered over to the small box fridge. He was hoping that his current position on the board game of life, would give him a good roll. It did. He discovered the glass bottles of Coke resting on the fridge shelf. He poured the sugary contents out and filled the bottle with the alcohol. He searched the desk for matches and found a box in the bottom drawer. He stuffed the paper towels, from atop the fridge, into the neck of the bottle. Limping, and carrying the bottle, he made his way towards the exit. Once outside he saw the woman in the car trying to make her escape. The Engelmann held her captive. Its appendages enclosing the axel of the vehicle. The haunted tree did not notice Clive. He ignited the Coke bottle. He watched the orange color burn on the paper towel stuffed in its glass neck. He chucked the bottle through the air. The bottle collided with its target, igniting the Engelmann on fire. Instantly the limbs broke free of the car. The tree sizzled; its branches flailed in the air as it timbered over onto the ground. The woman sped off, leaving Clive watching the tree go up in smoke. This would surely be the greatest story to tell Hugh the next time he visited the cemetery.

Clive went back inside and brought out another homemade Molotov. He broke it over the tree. A wail of agony rose from the tree and traveled in the smoke. The cry sent a sensation that rattled Clive's bones. He collapsed next to the burning plant. His mind raced, searching for any logical answer to this insanity. Maybe insanity did not need understanding. That was the single reassurance insanity had to offer, *chaos, plain and simple.* His buddy of two years shot at least forty people. What would drive someone to do that? No, he knew what Eli believed about such things. Eli's admission ticket had ended. This was his final move on the board game of life. He played and was dealt.

Now Clive was freezing in a blood-stained elf suit, next to a burning, possessed tree. Surely that woman would call the police. Once she hit the open road, she could find help. He hoped that the little girl would be saved. He laid patiently thinking of roads and how maybe if he would have driven down a different one he would not be here, half-dead in the snow. Half dead? Well, that ain't bad.

The sirens came around half an hour later. The smell of decaying flesh poisoned the air. Clive was lifted onto a stretcher and into the back of a blinking ambulance. He saw the Engelmann smoldering and crackling still. He began to panic on the stretcher.

"Don't put the fire out! Don't put the tree"- but he saw men start to extinguish it, then the doors were slammed shut. The ambulance sped him away to his salvation. Much later in the week, when the tide drifted back out to a calm sea, when the blood stained plaza fell back into a legendary act of terrorism, Clive learned that forty-eight people had perished. Sixteen of those dead were children, the rest adults. On top of the deaths, another ten adults were critically injured. The little girl with the blue eyes survived. So did the woman. They both came to Clive while he was in the hospital. They agreed not to speak of the tree, and they agreed Eli had done it all.

Sometime later in the following year, well into January, Clive was once again visiting Hugh in Lone Pine Cemetery. He closed his journal after finishing reading his story of the haunted Christmas Tree. He decided that Hugh had to be smiling there, under the ground. He looked up, surprised to see the woman from the plaza standing above him.

"Quite a story," she said.

"Hello," said Clive. "How long have you been standing there? What are you doing here?"

"I came to visit my father, whom Eli killed. Would you like to go get a drink? Or a bite?"

Clive looked into her big, oval, green eyes. He saw a road there that maybe he should take. Roads were meant to be traveled. He knew they all had road blocks, forks, baggage; they all had skeletons that hung in the closet. But something about those emerald shiny pupils prompted him to think that perhaps her skeletons could hang with his. After all, their first road trip had been a doozy. He got to his feet. They went for tea and sandwiches, and it was pleasant. It really was.

Road of Darkness

...Behold, I am against your magic bands which you hunt the souls like birds, and I will rip them from your arms, and I will let the souls you hunt go free... -Ezekiel 13:20

1.

It would begin in the dark like all things evil do: the lightless curtain that fell each night upon the Texan desert town of Shafter. This place was hardly a town, but a ghost town of spirits and ancient folklore. Still, Victoria Lopez was out in the Cibolo Creek; up to her waist in the water. A ghostly figure stood on the creek's edge watching her. In the pale moonlight she could see his hoofed legs. His stature was tall, his voice a hypnotic, deep rasp. She continued to hold her newborn under the water's surface. The tiny infant thrashed gently. Gentleness, the only thing a baby knew.

Victoria's long curly hair stuck to her face and neck. She listened carefully to what her visitor was instructing. "This is the way to the power. Offer me this sacrifice. Offer yourself to me and I will bring you great power. You will forever be bound to me. Your service and name will be included in this book."

The figure fell silent as Victoria stood. The infant's body stayed floating face down in its watery grave. She waded through the creek, which reflected the round white moon, and the face of a child murderer. She fell to her knees in front of the haunting man. The rest of her offspring (six to be exact) were piled next to the man; they were burning. She could see now that he wore a hood. From underneath the hood on his forehead were two large lumps.

"Do not gaze at me child!" he growled. "You have not earned that honor!"

Quickly, Victoria lowered her eyes to his feet. He placed a heavy hand on her shivering shoulder. She tried to hold back her cries, but the emotion burst forth, pouring down her face in waterfalls. "Do not cry my love. Your tears do no good. A deed is a deed, a bargain a deal. Here child. Sign your name." The sinister visitor handed her his book and a feather pen. "Use the quill to draw your blood and sign your name legibly on the line." Victoria stared at the feather. She knew exactly what she was doing. But her husband had been unfaithful, he struck her just last night. She would be weak, but with this new promise of power, she would get her revenge. She cut a thin line with the quill across her palm. The blood ran lightly, but there was enough to dip the writing utensil in its wetness. Without any more hesitation, she scribbled her name into his book. He snapped the book shut and pulled Victoria to her feet. His mouth was now on hers. Her lips spread and she felt a warm bumpy tongue enter. Joyfully it danced in her mouth, tasting like blood and ash. Then he was out of her, shoving her away. He soared up into the heavens leaving behind a confused Victoria.

A tingle spread from her mouth to her neck. She felt as if lightning had struck her. Her body shook violently, she could not calm her nervous system. Out from somewhere in the night an owl cried. The iconic hoot floated out under the stars. Then another hoot from somewhere close. She collapsed onto her back in a cloud of dust. Her body still writhing and contorting into weird positions on the sand. An owl landed on her chest; it was followed by another, until finally a parliament of owls accompanied her. Their oval, inky eyes bore into hers which were now fogging. Then all was calm, all was without light, and all was dead.

2.

Mark Fisher kept both his hazel eyes on the road before him. Its aging, cracked top beckoned him onward, like a broken kaleidoscope. The tar dancing with the yellow and white stripes reminded Mark of the famous Yellow Brick Road that had led a little girl with red shoes to a fantasy land. The current road he was on, however, was leading him and his wife from Marfa, Texas, to Mexico for a much needed vacation and visit to the in-laws. Maria

Gutierrez (now Fisher) smiled at her husband. He returned a grin and glanced in his rearview. Four-month -old Antonio was fast asleep in the backseat of the Kia sedan. The green guardians of the road reflected back to him in his headlights. The sign read twenty-five miles to Shafter.

"I hate that town," Maria replied, leaning her head back on the seat. "It's especially scary at night."

Mark contemplated this. "We have to stop. I do need gas. I still don't understand all the superstition around here."

His wife turned in her seat, a look of concern gripped her face. "My people take our heritage and legends seriously."

"Your people?" Mark laughed.

"We are stopping for gas, but that's it. Shafter is like what? Population thirty? It is a ghost town and for good reason. Many wars were fought on this soil. Many perished. It has been said that their ghostly bodies still walk the desert in search of rest. There are also legends of animals that are part man part beast. It is best if we do not speak their names," said Maria.

"La Llorona, Chupacabra," said Mark, smiling.

"No digas esos nombres, idiota!" yelled Maria.

"Now babe, you know I only understood half of what you said."

She glared at him, her brown eyes now furious with fire. "Let me guess, you understood the idiot part."

"Sí."

Antonio awoke from his slumber. He stirred in his car seat, letting soft whimpers escape his mouth. The whimpers turned into cries. Maria leaned into the back seat, comforting the child. He was in an all-white jumper, painted with dinosaurs of all shapes and colors. Easily he returned to his dreams with the Sandman as Maria rubbed his tiny feet.

"We really do have a great child. I love you," she said. Mark cranked his head over to her, and kissed her on the lips. "Love you too, mi amor." The sedan rolled into a lousy, local-owned gas station. As Mark sat there squeezing the wheel, he felt an uneasiness spread over him. But they were just stories and stories never hurt anyone.

3.

In a sweater and jean pants, Mark got out of the Kia, and headed across to the gas station. The name of the place was in Spanish, and Mark didn't even bother with trying to pronounce it. A chilled wind swept around him, tossing trash and a foul odor over the pumps. The building was a small, blue-crested rectangle. Lampposts stationed around the business guided him as he entered the store. Once inside, the lights were much brighter. Racks filled with various candies and snacks tempted him. Ignoring temptation, he walked through the store and up to the clerk. He was an older gentleman dressed in dirty overalls with a rosary hanging around his neck and a nametag that read Juan.

"Buenas noches, Señor. Como puedo ayudarte?"

Mark stared at him. He knew he had said goodnight, or good evening. But what the hell was at the end of that sentence? He tried hard to remember some of the words his wife had taught him. He loved Mexican culture; he harbored no ill feelings to his brothers from behind the fence across the Rio Grande. He rubbed his lips with his right hand. The clerk smiled.

"Baño?" asked Juan. Mark shook his head. The man laughed. "Drogas?"

"Oh, no! No!" exclaimed Mark, he knew that one for sure.

"Gas?" asked Juan.

"Sí, shit, you speak English?" cried Mark.

"Un poco, mi friend," he said, as Mark handed him forty dollars. The station had only two pumps and Juan glanced out the front checking for the Kia. "Gracias, Señor."

Mark nodded to the clerk and hurried back outside. He crossed over the smooth concrete reaching his car. The night mocked him from outside the bubble of light shining down from the lampposts. He unhooked the nozzle and started to feed his vehicle the much needed fuel. He peered inside to find Maria asleep. He took his head off the window and stared blankly at the numbers rising on the pump. Then, from somewhere on the wind, he heard a crying of sorts. The weeping was distinct, like that of a woman or small child. Entranced by this new sound, he followed it away from the pump and behind the store.

He reached the back of the station and found no child or woman. The crying tone got louder and sounded farther out into the desert beyond the station. The wailing rose from somewhere out in the ocean of the desert. He continued in the direction of the cries, hoping to find its source.

4.

Mark fumbled around in the suffocating darkness. He stood in what he could tell was a field. Lindheimers Mulhy bushes congregated around him. The light protruding from his phone shone into the skinny stringy plants. The sad sobbing fell quiet, and all became calm. Then a rustling noise rose from the left of him. Then another rustle, until the noise surrounded him on all sides. He turned a three-sixty, trying to find who, or what, was near. After a few moments the new sound subsided and faded off. He was left listening to crickets and other nighttime singers. But then in the wink of an eye all fell still. He could only hear his own panting, his breaths tearing at his lungs. He had ventured far from the station; he could barely see the silhouette of the aging store, sitting beneath the lampposts. A force of wind swooped down onto his head. He crashed to the ground in fright. What seemed like an object fell onto him again and he realized it was some kind of bird. This time, sharp nails tore at his scalp. Something was attacking him.

The assailant did not screech or cry, but was a silent tormentor. Mark guessed it was a large bird. He bolted back across the field, kicking up sprays of sand. He was in decent shape for his age, but this was no advantage to him. The bird lunged down, grabbing him by the shoulders with its talons. These were not like any bird feet Mark had ever seen, they were different. They resembled human fingers. The phalanges were sharp and strong. The nails at the end, reached at least six inches and dug into the flesh of his shoulders. Yes, this was a very large bird indeed, at least four feet tall. Mark was uprooted from the earth, rising higher into the sky as the bird soared. Mark dropped his cellphone, watching it fall beneath his dangling feet. The light got smaller and smaller, until finally disappearing from sight. He felt warm blood drizzle down his shoulder blades and chest. He flew along in the deep sky until he was released from the grasp. He heard the creature screech, as he plummeted out of the clouds, falling into an abandoned water tower. The top had been destroyed by nature long ago, at the same time the very railroad beneath it, went out of commission. Mark fell freely into its steel belly, sending tremors down its wooden frame.

As Mark regained his breath, he saw an orange glow begin to form in the darkness around him. His tongue stuck to the roof of his mouth; he was mute, unable to speak at the growing orb. The light transformed into an opening. A scaly hand reached forth. Black nails that curled at the tips clutched the sides of the gaping orifice, expanding it. A body spilled from the burning orb, Mark felt the heat brush his face. A man stood to his feet, dressed in an onyx hood. His legs looked like a goat's. He had some sort of medieval weapon harnessed across his back. He reached for it, pulling it out from its straps. Mark saw from the glow of the flame that the man held a large scythe. Its razor edge glistened in the light of the fiery orb.

Before Mark could dispatch his tongue from his pallet, the man speared him through the neck, using the scythe. He picked Mark's body up, turning, walking back to the floating orb from where he came. Mark hung lifeless on the weapon. The orb devoured both men, leaving the water tower in quiet tranquility.

5.

Maria slept with her head back, mouth wide open; snoring softly. Her husband had insisted on driving at night due to less traffic. A thumping noise from the roof of her car awakened her from the dream state. She sniffed and stretched, looking about for her husband. He was not there, and the pump had stopped some minutes ago. The nozzle had already shut off and numbers stopped completely. She turned, checking on baby Antonio. He was fine, asleep in the car seat, drool building up on his lips. There was another thump from somewhere above her, when a man burst out of the doors of the station. He had a shotgun in his hands. She studied the man in a daze of fear and bewilderment. His name tag said Juan, and his face strained with concentration. He raised the weapon up at her sedan and fired. Three sounds followed: a bang as the gun was fired, and a screech followed by the sound of flapping. Juan ran towards her, she quickly rolled up the window in a panic. "Era un monstruo. Era La Lechuza!" screamed Juan. He danced frantically around the outside of the vehicle pointing in the sky. He was very short, and his bald head that housed only hair on the sides made Maria want to laugh, if she wasn't so scared. "Fallé!" he cried, "I missed." She rolled down the window a few inches. He finally calmed down and waited patiently on the other side of the car window. His brown eyes held fear, but she could tell he wasn't going to hurt her. "¿Que esta pasando? ¿Qué estás disparando? Dónde esta mi esposo?" she asked, inquiring about her husband.

"Mi no see him," said Juan. "I saved you. Aquí, ten esto. Te protegerá del monstruo." He reached into his overall pockets and revealed a rope with seven knots. He extended his arm towards Maria, wanting to give it to her, but the wild creature knocked into him sideways, sending him sprawling away from the car. The rope fell onto the seat. Maria screamed in horror as she stared into the Lechuza's face. The structure was shaped like a heart, and it resembled a Barn Owl but its features were different. The eyes were deeply inflamed with a glowing hint of ruby. The texture seemed leathery and her nose a beak. It was certainly an older woman. The hair was thick, long and full of aging grey. Maria realized she was staring at a half owl, half human woman. She stood about four feet high, with a wingspan of seven feet. Her wings quickly retreated inwards, collapsing on her nude body. The

Lechuza ripped the back door right off its hinges, and bobbed towards Antonio. Maria moved fast, grabbing the seven knotted rope. The Lechuza turned swiftly, pecking at Maria's forehead knocking her against the dashboard and drawing blood. The creature went in for another attack and Maria held up the rope. The Lechuza wailed and stopped her assault. She returned her attention to Antonio. The owl-woman ripped the infant from the vehicle, with him still in the car seat. Strands of the nylon seatbelt trailed out from behind, as the Lechuza rose into the sky with its captive. Maria screamed and climbed into the driver's seat. She saw Juan running towards her with two white bags in his hands; his shotgun dancing on a strap hanging from his chest. He climbed into the Kia. "¡De prisa! Vamonos. A la torre de agua," he replied. She floored the pedal, almost sending it through the frame of her car. "Tower?" she asked. Juan nodded his head as he gazed at her. He smirked. "Sí, señora. The water tower."

6.

Maria sped through the night as fast as the Kia would permit, her face set on the road before her, trying to remember what side street to exit. Everyone from Marfa, Texas and south, knew of Shafter being haunted. She had grown up with stories about the legend that she now was chasing. There had been two tales her abuela would always tell her, if she misbehaved. "Now Maria, you go to sleep right now, or the Llorona will get you," her grandmother used to say. "Finish the quehaceres, or the Llorona will snatch you up tonight." Of course being so impressionable, young Maria believed her grandma. When her teenage years came, her grandmother changed it to the Lechuza. The story went that a woman who had been beaten by her lover and been faithful to the same unfaithful abusing man, sold her soul to the Devil. She had killed her seven children as payment to the Devil. In so doing, she thought that he would bestow great powers to her. Powers to exact her revenge. The Llorona legend was similar in almost every way, except it was believed that the Lechuza was also part witch, part owl. The Llorona was only to be thought of as a ghost.

As she drove, Maria entertained the idea that myths turned into legends; legends into traditions. Well not now, most certainly not now. She let her eyes wander over to Juan. His gun sat barrel up, resting between his legs. He wasn't sitting but crouching, his head stretching out the window as he gazed up into the sky. "Why the salt and rope?" she asked, elevating her voice so he could hear her. "Qué?" he inquired as he pulled himself inward. She looked at him thoughtfully. "Por qué la sal y la cuerda?" she asked again. He smiled; this time he almost chuckled.

"Seven niños, siete deaths. La sal la quemará," he answered. Maria nodded, returning her eyes to the ever reaching road. She felt positive despite the circumstances she found herself in. She had no idea where Mark had gone. But since this creature had become known, chances are he had met her, and their meeting was not one of joyfulness. Despite this, a confidence had started to brew within her. Perhaps this loco Juan would prevail. Antonio was flying somewhere in the stars. They had to get him back! She knew they would. They neared the water tower, and Juan made her park a few yards off. With the sky changing into day, they did not see any trace of the fabled creature. There was a ladder stationed on the side of the tower. Juan mounted it, surprised to see Maria trying to follow. He paused, glaring down on her. "No, too dangerous!" he exclaimed. Maria progressed without hesitation. "That is my child, I'm doing this!" she shouted. Juan started back down the ladder, Maria dismounted, letting him pass. Together they huddled underneath the wooden legs of the structure.

"This is where el Diablo is," said Juan, holding onto his shotgun as if it were a lightsaber. "I know, where she meets the Devil," replied Maria. "What do we do now?" Juan looked at her for a few seconds. "You climb, I shoot," he replied. He handed her the seven knotted rope and a bag of salt. She pocketed the rope; holding tightly to the salt as she started her ascent up the ladder.

7.

The Lechuza glided through the clouds with grace. Purple beams pierced the sky. Dawn was coming. The creature knew she must reach the water tower before the sun hung high in the sky. Her master only walked at night. He would not accept her offering of the child if there was sunlight. She dipped downward out of the clouds, astonished to see the infant's mother climbing the water tower. The Lechuza circled twice, trying to locate the man. When she could not find him, she dived into the water tower screeching, beckoning her master. She landed inside, softly putting the baby down. She made sure he was unharmed and then rose out of the metallic belly. She would have to act fast to eradicate this nuisance of a mother.

She swooped downward, talons out, into the woman on the ladder. It was a solid strike, ripping the woman's jacket; causing her to lose her position on the ladder. Somehow though, the woman remained holding on; her grip solid, swinging her body back up and continuing onward. The owl-woman hooted in amazement and prepared for another attack. This time, right before her claws struck the mother, Maria flung her arm outward, releasing some sort of powder or sand. When the substance hit the Lechuza, the creature screamed in agony. Her prey had a weapon and it was salt. The substance left burn marks on the legs and stomach of the Lechuza. From her beak, a fierce scream of rage erupted, she dived once more aiming for the mother's head. Suddenly, a bullet flew into her path of travel, causing the bird-woman to evade. The Lechuza maneuvered quickly, rising away from the water tower.

Maria picked up her pace, after she heard the second bang of Juan's shotgun. She had only a few more feet until the top. Once there she guessed she would jump down into the center of the tower. It was at least ten or twelve feet, but she didn't know how else to get in. Her back stiffened with pain, she could feel the lines of blood caressing down towards her waist. The creature had got her good. She felt as if a million bees had stung her. She continued upward, gaining more rungs on the ladder. Finally she perched at the top. She peered into the tower and gasped.

A fiery orb began to present itself out of the shadows. It grew larger in size with each second she watched. A tall figure wearing a hood, emerged from the orb. He had a scythe slung on his back and something hung on his waist. It seemed to be three objects, but Maria could not make them out. She heard Antonio start to cry and the figure did too, and he headed towards her child. With what strength she had left, she leapt from the rim of the tower, descending directly on top of the hooded man. Both parties fell to the ground in a dusty swirl.

8.

Juan hustled across the desert field. The Lechuza squawked at him from above. He fell to the ground as she tackled him. Clouds of dirt engulfed them. The shotgun flew from his hands and he now wrestled with the fabled creature. Her wings closed around him, but her tiny hands at the top of the wing were weak. He easily blocked her attempts. Finally she pushed away from him and flew back up into the air. He was bleeding from his chest and face, but he still had the salt. The atmosphere became tainted in an orange glow. The desert was awakening. He spied the Kia and made his way towards it, hoping to find refuge beneath the vehicle. He reached the car and threw himself under it, his legs sticking out only for a moment. But that moment was all the Lechuza needed. Using her talons with human-finger-like grip, she grabbed Juan's ankles and pulled him out from underneath. In his mind he started to pray, but he was still flung about fifteen feet away from the car.

The Lechuza dived again, this time penetrating Juan right in the stomach. The owl-woman pinned him on the ground, standing on top of him. She started to peck away at his face. Juan quickly pulled the bag from the inside of his overalls and tossed the contents out. It sprayed all over the Lechuza. The salt covered most of her lower body and then in a final thrust, Juan disposed the rest onto her incoming face. The Lechuza went in for another pecking, but was met with extreme burning. Her talons broke free from Juan as she toppled over next to him, writhing in pain.

The shadows seeped away as the sun rose higher. They quickly withdrew as the light chased after them. Inside the water tower, Maria rolled off the hooded man and tried to scream. To her horror, not a sound escaped her throat. The man had small bumps protruding out of his head, almost like horns. His chest was beefy and built solid. His lower body was that of a goat. Around his waist hanging on his rope-like belt were three heads. One head was that of her husband. Immediately she sprinted away from the man, towards her baby. She positioned herself over the crying infant. "You cannot have him!" she roared. The hooded Devil smiled. "I take what I please. This is the law. The deal from the beginning of time."

Maria was desperate; she had only a bag of salt. What defense was that against a monster from the netherworlds? The Devil walked slowly towards Maria. He raised his scythe off his back; holding it in his mighty arms. "Now I will have been awarded three offerings tonight. She has done well," he said, as he held the weapon up in the air. Maria braced herself for the strike, trying her best to shield Antonio. The hit however did not come. Sunlight arrived, erasing the columns of shadows. The dark figure growled as he was sucked back into the burning orb, for the keepers of the dark still have rules to adhere to. Then everything was bright; everything was becoming serene. Recognizing his mother, Antonio fell silent as she scooped him up into her arms. She was not sure how to escape from this metallic stomach, but then saw a drainage hatch with another ladder. With the baby zipped up in her jacket and holding him with one arm, she descended back down the tower. Maria made it safely to the ground. Antonio had started to cry, but she had found his favorite pacifier in her pocket and put it into his mouth. He would be content for now. Maria limped across the field, almost tripping over the old railroad tracks. Here she saw Juan lying motionless, blood spattered across his front. When she got closer she saw a beautiful, older, Mexican woman, naked, lying a few feet from him. Her body bore deep sizzling burn marks. The wounds were still smoking from her flesh. Maria located her Kia that sat another ten yards away. She looked down at Juan, a little light left in his eyes. Light. That was good. The light had extinguished the blackness.

Maria gazed upon the dying clerk from the rundown gas station. She smiled at him, so thankful for his actions. His eyes, turning into smaller slits, moved up to meet hers. She took his hand. "Ahora estoy con Dios," he said. "You go with God now." His eyelids fell shut and his body went limp. In tears Maria went to her vehicle. There was no car seat now, but that did not matter. She strapped Antonio in as best she could. Sobbing and trying to gain composure, she climbed into the driver's seat. To her gratefulness, the Kia started. The sun was bright as she drove out of the field, headed back to the main road. She found her cellphone and tried calling for help. There was no signal. She decided to leave the bodies behind. She did not see a point in driving around with dead bodies. She was scared and tired. At the next town she would find help. Maria had no idea on how to explain to anyone the supernatural events that occurred just under eight hours ago. She hoped they would believe it. She sped up the car, contemplating this thought. Legends were told for a reason and legends never die. As the desert came to life around her, welcoming a new day, a new time to make new choices and choose hope, Maria wondered what kind of funeral she should have for her husband. Life was cruel. There was no denying that. Was that the joke of life? Strife, suffering until the coffin was nailed shut? Maria did not want to think with such negativity. But the night had been filled with suffering. Dying was unavoidable. Antonio giggled from beside her, breaking her thoughts. She finally felt a smile form on her lips. A child's laughter was like a heavenly choir of angels. There was still so much life to be lived behind that small giggle. She knew, like all humans do, that we were all going to live, and all going to die. Legends to some, myths to others. It was a strange omniscient feeling, waiting for the end.

Epilogue

I see the graves all around me
Who am I that I stand
Among them?
The bodies lay at my feet
Like distant memories
Apparitions stare back at me
As the soil
Buries the depravity
The torture lingers
This suffering of eternal slumber.

A letter to the reader

Dear reader, congratulations are in order. You have made it to the very end of the book. You have survived each entry in *Dead Diaries.* Yes, take a deep breath and slow your heart. All is calm, all is right. To be completely honest, this is the most comfortable I have been in my writing in a very long time. I hope that I have frightened you in such a way that you would find me quite provocative and polarizing. This book came about as a way of entertainment with brief dark humor. Even if that satire was bleak. As of writing this, I started on this book in November of 2016. I finished it in May 2017. My journey through this book led me to discover some startling ideas and stories based within places I have traveled. Almost all of the places I wrote about here, I have visited. I especially loved St. Augustine, Florida, and Massachusetts.

In writing horror, I tried to stay to my own idea of principals. To keep the story grounded in some type of reality, to make strong characters that have a fighting chance, and lastly; not make it too corny. Horror to me, is not what is on the other side of the door, but the journey it takes to open it. We all know what's on the other side, but it is within the plot, the narrative of the tale that hooks you. I believe that I have hooked you deep with this one. But you are free now, free to go back into the pond. But remember to watch out for The Frogman. If you are being cast back into a river, make sure you swim against the others. For there is nothing special about swimming the same way as everyone else. All quotes are the property of their respective owners. They were used for research purposes and to set the stage of each entry. They were found online at brainyquote.com. Cover photo was found on Pixabay.com under Public Domain. So dear reader, thank you for consuming this story. Until we meet again, farewell, and try to stay away from cemeteries or beef stands.

Austin German

About the author

Austin German has been writing stories ever since grade school. Winning in a poetry contest in sixth-grade, Austin realized his love for words. As his craft matured, he found inspiration from his love of all things horror and science fiction. He resides in the southwest region of Arizona with his german shepherd, Titan. He frequently travels to Colorado, Massachusetts and California. Austin's other work *"Perennial Harvest"* is also available on Createspace.com and Amazon.com.

23134822R00121

Made in the USA
Columbia, SC
06 August 2018